Living on Sisu

The 1913 Union Copper Strike Tragedy

Deborah K. Frontiera

The ABC's Press
Houston, Texas
2009

Copyright © 2009 by Deborah K. Frontiera

Second Printing, 2013

ISBN# 978-0-9820278-5-1
LCCN# 2008944223

Publisher's Cataloging-in-Publication data

Frontiera, Deborah K.
    Living on sisu : the 1913 Union Copper Strike tragedy / Deborah K. Frontiera.
        p. cm.
    ISBN 978-0-9820278-5-1
1. Copper Miners' Strike, Mich., 1913-1914—Fiction. 2. Copper mines and mining -- Michigan -- Fiction. 3. Finnish Americans -- Great Lakes Region (North America) -- Fiction. 4. Copper miners -- Great Lakes Region (North America) -- History -- Fiction. 5. Historical fiction.   I. Title.
PZ7.F92035 Li 2009
[Fic]—dd22   2008944223

Project Coordinator — Rita Mills
Cover Design — Gladys Ramirez
Text Design — Rita Mills
Editor — Faye Walker

Special photo note: the initial "N" following any of photo used indicates that J. W. Nara, grandfather of Dr. Robert Nara, was the photographer. According to Dr. Nara, it is highly likely that J.W. Nara took the other photos as well. J.W. Nara imprinted many of his photos with his mark, but not all of the thousands of photos he took were marked in this way. Of the unmarked photos which have become part of several collections and archives, the chances are perhaps ninety percent that they are Nara photos, especially those taken of the Calumet area.

To see more Nara photos depicting life in the Copper Country during the early 1900's, consider purchasing Deborah K. Frontiera's book, *Copper Country Chronicler: The Best of J. W. Nara.*

Printed in the United States of America

This book is dedicated to all those who lived and died that year, to the young people of today and tomorrow, so they will know what it was like, and to my grandchildren: present—Hailey Wilhelm and James Bonilla—and future . . .

Thank You

P eople to whom the author gives her most sincere thanks for their help in making this book as realistic as possible:

Dr. Robert Nara and Ruth Nara for their help and encouragement during production of the book;

James Kurtti, director of the Finnish American National Historic Archive and Museum, and editor of *The Finnish American Reporter*;

Abby Sue Fisher, Chief of Museum, Archives and Historical Services, Keweenaw National Historical Park;

Jay Rowe, Chairman of the 2004 Copper Country Homecoming and Old Settlers' Ball, historian and local expert on Cornish immigrants;

Will Shapton, historian for "Traditions Alive" of the Keweenaw Krayons service organization, Mohawk, MI;

Mrs. Mary Butina, Painesdale, MI, daughter of a 1913 striking miner and survivor of the Italian Hall Disaster (Age 97 when she interviewed with the author during the summer of 2003);

Richard Taylor, Houghton County Historical Society President;

Myrtle Barrette, local columnist and resident of Swedetown, MI;

Bill Baccus, dairy farmer, Traprock Rd., Lake Linden, MI;

Nancy Lamppa Wenberg, friend who makes *juustoa* and other traditional Finnish foods;

Debra Snow, MA, Director of Trauma Resources, on-line Help Desk, The Sidran Institute, a nonprofit organization devoted to helping people who have experienced traumatic life events.

The Finnish word "sisu" does not have an exact English translation. It might be defined as a quality people have giving them the courage, determination, and strength to make it through life's most difficult situations, or (as defined by Dr. Robert Nara) "a characteristic that takes over when determination and fortitude run out."

————◆————

Introduction

I grew up in Lake Linden. My father, Clarke Olson, taught math and mining engineering at Michigan Technological University. My grandfather, Louis Chester Pearce, grew up in Lake Linden. He graduated from the same high school that my mother, brother, sisters, and I did various years later. Chester graduated from the Michigan College of Mines (later re-named Michigan Technological University). He and my grandmother, Jessie Otto Pearce, lived in the mining regions of Mexico the first several years after they married. They were not in the Copper Country at the time of the 1913 strike, but returned to Lake Linden a year or so later when my grandfather began working in his father's hardware store and helping with other business interests.

I can't begin to count the number of times while growing up that some teacher, parent or other adult shook a finger at a group of children with the warning, "Never yell 'fire' in a crowded room!" During most of my school years, the C&H whistle blowing at the end of the day shift was as familiar a sound as the voices of my friends. I remember clearly the concern of classmates whose fathers worked at the stamp mill when C&H closed in 1968.

I never really appreciated my heritage until I reached adulthood. Employment opportunities took my husband and our children from Michigan to Colorado, then to Kansas, and finally to Texas in 1985. We returned to Lake Linden often on summer vacations and took our children to the local museums and to our favorite beaches on Lake Superior.

In 1998, we bought a cottage on Rice Lake, nine miles from Lake Linden, and began to spend our summers there. The idea of writing a story about the strike of 1913 from a young person's point of view came to me the summer that a friend and I attended the premier of the opera, *Children of the Keweenaw*, at the restored Calumet Theater. I bought my copy of *Rebels on the Range* that night. I spent the next few summers reading books and historical documents on file at the agencies listed, talking to local historical experts, walking the streets of Calumet, sitting inside restored churches, hiking from the top of the hill in Swedetown to Kearsarge Street in Laurium, getting to know "Emma" and her world, and gaining a sincere appreciation for those who lived and worked in the mines during the early twentieth century.

—Deborah K. Olson Frontiera

Living on Sisu

The 1913 Union Copper Strike Tragedy

Emma Niemi, her family, and friends in *Living on Sisu* are fictional characters. The Calumet and Hecla Mining Company (usually referred to as C&H) and the strike of 1913 were, sadly, very real. Emma's experiences are as close to what it may have been like for a young person as research can make them. A list of historical people can be found in the Appendix, along with acknowledgments of resource people, photo credits, and a list of references. The historical photographs included are to give the reader a sense of time and place. The names of most people in the photographs (unless the captain refers to historical people) are unknown and should only be considered to be "like" the fictional characters.

A typical Finnish family, not exactly like Emma's family, but this is how most Finnish families looked when having a formal portrait done.

Photo FAHA

A girl like Emma dressed for high school graduation. In the story, Emma has not reached this age.

Photo FAHA

1913

Thursday, May 1

I am twelve years old today. It has been a wonderful day. Even the sun helped, and it was most welcome. Winter is always long in Michigan's Upper Peninsula, but this year it seemed especially so because we had snow and sleet even in April. At school today, we danced around the May Pole. I was right next to my best friend, Marie Beauchamp. We laughed and laughed as we passed our ribbons over and under each other's with the rest of the sixth grade girls. At lunch, we talked of things we will try to do together when school is out in June.

The best part came this evening. Mama had supper ready, as she always does when my father, my brother Jaako and Juhani Hakala, who is also from Finland and boards with us, come home from pushing tram cars in the Calumet and Hecla copper mines. Papa went upstairs first, something he does not usually do. When he came down, he handed me a packet and said, "Happy Birthday, my not-so-little New American girl. Here is something you can write down more of those ideas in—the ideas you get so many A's for in school. Always stay in school and learn even more. That is the best thing you can give yourself or your family."

He said it in Finnish, but I have put what it means in English. He always calls me his "New American girl" because I was the first of my family to be born an American citizen and in the first year of a new century. Papa says in Finland they celebrate a child's name day, the day of baptism, rather than a birthday. So we celebrate my brothers' name days because they were born in Finland, but my sisters' and my birthdays because we were born in America, where birthdays are the thing to celebrate.

The packet was wrapped in brown paper from the grocery store and tied with a piece of twine. I opened it and there lay this journal, two pencils, a penknife to sharpen them and a rubber eraser! It is much more than I ever expected for a gift. There is never much extra money in our family, and what there is always goes into Mama's jar on the top shelf of the pantry for Papa to buy a farm.

"It is a good year," Mama said, also in Finnish. "You are almost through with grade school and nearly a young lady."

Jaako, Mattii, Jenni and Katri all clapped for me. Mr. Hakala gave me a pat on the back. Mama's fish *mojakka* was especially good because the stew was made from fresh fish, not smoked fish like we had all winter. We had *marjavelia* for dessert. Mama made it from a jar of last summer's raspberries.

Katri looked at the fruit sauce. "I thought we ate all the raspberries," she said.

"I hid the last jar," Mama told her, "to save it for Emma's birthday."

Jenni and Katri (who are nine and seven years old) are already asleep in our bed. The front windows of our house at the very end of Tunnel Street in Swedetown face nothing but another row of company houses. I am glad my upstairs window looks west across the meadow to the forest. As I watched the sky change from red and orange to lavender, I could still hear Mama, Papa and Mr. Hakala talking in the kitchen.

Mr. Hakala said the man from the Western Federation of Miners talked to him again today, and asked him if he would join. He asked Papa what he planned to do. Papa said what he always does, "I don't want to join that union. I don't hold with their socialist ideas. Besides, I put up with this job almost thirteen years now. I can stand it another six months until we have all our land money."

Mr. Hakala said, "That's all well and good, but what about me? I'm just starting out. I have saved barely enough money to bring my wife and son to America. My son is tiny. There is no one to work but me."

Papa told Mr. Hakala he has to decide for himself.

Mr. Hakala raised his voice a little and said, "Yes, but if we don't all stick together, none of us will ever get anything. C&H won't listen as long as it's only a few."

It is the same talk almost every night. Papa always says he just wants to get out. It makes me tired and confused.

Now, here I sit at the window. It is almost dark. I

— 5 —

make this promise to myself for Papa: I will always use my very best English grammar in this journal as my teachers tell me, and I will get as much education as I can.

Friday, May 2

Winter might finally be over, but it was not much above freezing when the mine whistle blew at seven o'clock. Jenni and Katri and I slept all curled up together with two quilts over us. We did not want to get out of bed, but I had to get up. It is my job to take the chamber pots to the outhouse and bring in another bucket of water. Although the big red water tower on our hill helps give our homes good water, we do not have pipes inside the house. A pump at the edge of our garden brings us water from the town's pipes.

The men ate eggs and bacon and walked to the mine shaft before we woke. My sisters and I had *juustoa* and *korppua*, oven cheese and toast. I dunked my *korppua* in coffee now that Mama lets me have some. My sisters dunked theirs in hot milk. Jenni and Katri helped Mama wash the dishes. They have only a short walk to Swedetown's school. I must walk much farther to my school because Swedetown's school has only grades one through five. First, I always take our cow Daisy across the street to the town pasture.

At school, my teacher praised my essay again, and asked me to read it aloud. James Richards, who sits right behind me, whispered, "Teacher's pet! You think you're smart, but you're just a dumb Finn." Then he put the tip of my braid into his ink well.

I felt my face and neck get hot. Then he whispered, "There's a little red in your neck. You must be a Red Finn," and snickered. He always does something mean if I get a better grade. I said nothing to my teacher because I have enough trouble from him without being called a tattletale as well. I would like to stick my foot out and trip him the next time he walks by. Five weeks and I will be rid him and his friends.

Lunch is always the same at school. We all sit in our little groups—James and his ilk, the Poles and Slavs together, the Italians, we Finnish from Swedetown, and so forth. It is strange how Marie and I, a Finn and a French girl, ended up together. It was at the start of the school year. The boys were picking on her because she was new and did not know much English. I could not stand it. I told them we should all just get along.

They yelled, "Greenhorn and dumb Finn," at both of us as I led her to where I was sitting.

The others from Swedetown began to ignore me because I befriended someone who isn't Finnish. With my help, her English is pretty good now and we are happy being friends.

After school, Daisy was very stubborn on the way back from the pasture. I think she wanted to stay and eat all that nice fresh grass after a winter of hay. Her milk and Mama's *viiliä*, or cultured milk, taste better when she eats fresh grass.

When I finally got into the house, there sat Jenni's teacher in our parlor.

"Guess what!" Jenni said, "It's our turn to have Miss Prince stay with us." I greeted Miss Prince politely but sighed to myself. I know it is necessary, but I hate our turn to have one of the teachers at our house. It means we girls must give up our room and sleep on a pallet on the floor in my parents' room. I wonder if Miss Prince doesn't like being in different houses much either. She has no place to call home.

I barely got to eat my supper since I must always translate for my parents and Mr. Hakala.

"Emma," Miss Prince said, "I heard you won your school essay contest. Please, tell me about what you wrote."

"We had to choose some recent news and tell what we thought about it," I told her. I explained how, last February, I read in the newspaper about a state representative who had introduced a law not to cut so many trees from the forests here. Then in March one representative spoke before the Michigan Senate to ask them to pass the law. The law only went to some committee and never was considered. There are too many people who think we must have even more industry and that there is no end to the forests. I had written my essay about what the representative said and how I thought he was right. I also wrote that there must be someone smart enough to find a way to have industry and forests together.

"Your parents must be very proud of you," Miss Prince said.

There was all the usual conversation about the weather, how hard the work is in the mines, and Papa's hope to buy land. He said he has his eye on a piece in the Trap Rock Valley that has some meadow and some forest. We Finnish people call the Trap Rock Valley *Karjala*, like the *Karjala* in Finland where our national epic poetry, *The Kalevala*, was written.

"Meadow for crops and cows. Trees to cut for a house," Papa said. "And enough land for all my sons." He said "all" very loud because he was a second son, with no land to inherit in Finland.

Sometimes I get tired of translating so much, but then I remind myself maybe God made me good at both English and Finnish so I can help people understand each other. Would that make people like James Richards not hate us so much?

⇒◆⇐

Today Calumet celebrated Mother's Day. It is so odd that there is no "town" called Calumet, but the whole area of Red Jacket, Yellow Jacket, Blue Jacket and other mine locations, and Laurium together, is all called Calumet. At services, our pastor had all the mothers and grandmothers stand up. He said a special prayer for them, and for all those who wore white flowers because their mothers are in heaven.

As we walked back from the National Lutheran Church, I watched for Marie like I always do. She usually waits for me at the corner of Sixth and Scott Street, close to St. Anne's where she goes to church. We went into the meadows to pick flowers for my mama and hers, but there were not many because the spring has been so cold. Maybe there will be more next Sunday, the day Governor Ferris has declared will be Mother's Day in Michigan. We sat down to talk.

"One time I asked Papa why there are so many different churches around here," I said to Marie. "He said everybody likes to go with their own countrymen so they can hear their own language."

"Sometimes my parents tell me we shouldn't be

friends," she said, "because Catholics are the only ones who will go to heaven."

"My parents say Catholics worship statues."

"That's not true."

"I know," I said. "Everybody talks, but nobody listens. Let's not ever let what anybody says keep us from being friends."

She took my hand and put it to her heart. "Friends for always," she said.

I took her hand and put it on my heart and said, "Friends forever."

If Emma and her family walked down Sixth Street and looked to their right while crossing Oak St., this is what they would have seen. The church in the background is St. Joseph's (later renamed St. Paul the Apostle in 1966).
Photo MTU-N

Sunday, June 1

Finally, my sisters and I have our room back. Since our family has two children at Swedetown's school, we must host a teacher for a full month instead of two weeks. Mama needed more help with the cooking, cleaning, and washing, so I had no time to be alone.

Mama seemed so sad all day, but she did not look like she wanted me to ask her about it. I finally asked Papa why when he was sitting on the front steps in the evening. He sighed and then said, "This would have been Iisakki's fifteenth *Iisakinpäivä*." (His name day.)

Iisakki was my brother who died very young. "Please tell me more about him," I said, "Mama does not like to."

Papa looked down at the ground and then he finally told me about when our family came to America.

Since Papa had no land of his own, he was a tenant farmer. The owner of the manor died and his son kicked everybody off the land. Papa had no way to support Mama and my brothers. He had good standing with his church so he was able to get a passport before the *rovasti,* a religious official in the state church, who read the conscription act of the Tsar of Russia. All unemployed men were to be rounded up and sent to fight for the Tsar, because Russia still ruled Finland.

Mama and Papa sold everything they had to buy passage to America. They sailed first to Liverpool, England, and from there to New York. Crossing the Atlantic as passengers in steerage was dreadful. The air was foul. A late winter storm came up and everybody got sick. Jaako and Matti were six and four then. Iisakki was only two. He got a fever and died. The ship captain buried him at sea the day before they landed in New York.

The Finnish agent in New York told Papa about good jobs in the Michigan copper mines. Papa, Mama, and my brothers arrived at the Calumet station with nothing but their bundles of clothes. Uno and Eva Aittamaa took us in until Papa had worked long enough to buy a few furnishings. The mine captain liked the fact that Papa was willing to work longer that the usual ten hours, so he recommended our family for the company house we still live in.

"Your Mama is sad every year on *Iisakinpäivä*," Papa said. "She always says that if God had to take him from us, at least it could have been someplace where she could visit his grave." Papa patted my back. "And then He gave us you."

The air had gotten too cold by then to enjoy being outside so we went in. I came up to sit by my window and watch the sunset. Now I realize why Mr. and Mrs. Aittamaa are still our family's best friends and why Papa took in Juhani Hakala. He has been with us two years now and it feels like he is part of the family. This has been Papa's way of giving back what the Aittamaa's gave us.

—◆◆◆—

Mama asked me to come straight home because Mrs. Aittamaa was coming with someone who doesn't speak Finnish.

When I came in, Mama was pouring coffee into her best cups—the four china ones that have saucers to match. She uses them only for very special company. Papa gave them to her for their wedding anniversary when I was just a baby. Mama asked me to help her carry them. Mrs. Aittamaa was sitting on our sofa in the parlor with another lady. I set down the tray to hand them their cups. Mrs. Aittamaa stood up and introduced me.

"Emma, this is Mrs. Annie Clemenc," she said.

Mrs. Clemenc stood and reached her hand out to me. She is by far the tallest woman I have ever seen. "I'm pleased to meet you, Emma," she said. "Mrs. Aittamaa told me about your prize-winning essay. Congratulations." I felt hot around my ears. I am sure my face turned red as a radish. Mrs. Clemenc took my hand in both of hers. Her hands were warm and rough from hard work like Mama's. She wore her brown hair all rolled up on top of her head, instead of a coiled braid like Mama's, so she seemed even taller. "Everybody calls me 'Big Annie,' and you can, too," she said. Her smile made me tingle clear down to my toes.

While the ladies sipped their coffee and ate Mama's toasted cinnamon bread, I was busy translating. Big Annie has organized the Ladies' Auxiliary No. 15 of the Western Federation of Miners. Mrs. Aittamaa joined and asked Mama to join.

"My husband does not like the WFM," Mama said. "He is not so sure about some of their ideas."

Mrs. Aittemaa told Mama, "You must not judge the whole union because a few of the people in it are socialists. Most of the men are not like that, and the Ladies' Auxiliary is a separate organization. We help and support the union but we are not actually part of it."

Big Annie and Mrs. Aittamaa talked back and forth about how important it was for everyone to stick together. "Like an *osuuskauppa*, a co-op," Mrs. Aittamaa said.

"Sometimes, we women have to give our men a little push in the right direction," Big Annie said.

Mama asked how much it would cost. "Don't worry about that," Mrs. Aittamaa said. "Just keep sending me a little of your good *juustoa*."

Mama smiled then and said she would join and go to the next meeting. She also said she would try to help Papa understand about the union.

<figure>—————◦————</figure>

We are out of school today. I like school, but I am still glad when summer comes. Marie and I will not be able to see each other as much though. Summer brings more chores like weeding the garden, canning the produce, picking wild berries . . . It seems there is always some job to be done. We will meet at our secret place in the meadow whenever we can. Matti finished his second year of high school today, too. Mama and Papa are proud that he has been able to stay in school. Jaako did not get to finish high school. As soon as he was 18 years old, he went to work with Papa to help save money for the land.

When Matti got home, he packed a small bag of extra clothes and caught the trolley down to Lake Linden. Mr. Lamppa, the farmer he worked for last summer, will pick him up at the trolley station. Matti will work all summer for him milking cows, making hay, and everything else on a farm. Mr. Lamppa will bring him home at the end of the summer with his pay—our winter supply of potatoes, onions, and hay for Daisy.

<figure>—————◦————</figure>

Saturday, June 7

What a treat tonight! Papa handed Mama forty cents to take Jenni, Katri, and me to the Bijou Theater. Last year, he let me go with Mama but this was the first time for Katri and Jenni. He said we should have a treat because we all got such good report cards. It was fun to watch the flickering pictures. It kept me busy though. I sat between Mama and Katri. I had to read the words on the screen for Katri and then say it in Finnish for Mama. Jenni can read it herself. It was a lot of whispering. I tried to be quiet enough not to bother the people around us. They did not complain so I guess I was all right. During some parts, everybody was laughing so loud. Mama and Katri could see what was funny without any words.

June evenings are so long that it was still light after the picture show ended. We walked in a wide line, all holding hands and still laughing over those silly Keystone Cops. I wish we had more evenings like this.

Monday, June 8

━━━◆◆◆━━━

Yesterday we began C&H's odd summer time. The company clocks are set ahead one half hour. So today, the morning shift started at 6:30 instead of 7:00. Company time will be 7:00 but the real time will be 6:30. They do that every summer because the sun rises so early. By changing our clocks and having the men start work half an hour early, they get home earlier and can enjoy the summer evenings. People who come here to visit must be very confused, but we get used to it after awhile.

Today's newspaper listed the free summer concerts by the C&H band. The first was tonight. It was outside near the Osceola Mine shaft. Mama and Papa were too tired to take us, but Papa promised we will go Friday when they perform the same music on the lawn near the C&H offices. I hope the weather is good.

Marie came running out to meet me in our pasture as I was fetching Daisy in the evening. "I'm sorry I can't come see you as much," she said. "My mother had her baby, and I must help take care of the house so she can rest."

"I understand," I told her. "Maybe you can go to the concert Friday, and we can sit together."

"Maybe," she said.

Daisy mooed very loud and pulled at her lead. Her udder was bulging. It sounded like she was saying, "Moooove ooooon! Milk me!"

Tuesday, June 10

T he WFM men came to visit Mr. Hakala and Papa
again tonight. Once again, Papa asked me to translate some of the things he does not understand.

"Four years ago," one of the men said, "we had
only a few members. Now we have nearly 7,000 across
the Copper Range. The WFM just won a raise to $3.00
a day for workers in Butte, Montana. Think how fast
you could get that land you want with fifty cents more
every day!"

"Didn't help Minnesota men much in '07," Papa
said. He continued in Finnish. "Even though I didn't go
to Hancock for the Red Flag parade to support them, I
got yelled at by all the captains. I am no socialist. I don't
want anybody to think I am. There is never a bit of red
anywhere in our house. *Ei yhtään!* Never!"

"Yes," the union man admitted. "Some of the
WFM's officers are socialists, but that is not what we
are all about. Back in 1907, we were a new union. We
didn't have enough support, so the strike failed. We
have a lot of members now."

Papa sighed. "I have enough trouble from this new
mine captain calling me a Red Finn. After he saw you

talking to me last time, he assigned my son and me to the worst stope in the lowest level."

Miners shoveling copper ore into a tram car. This is not a C&H mine and the side walls and ceiling, or "hanging wall" are shored up with more timbers than was typical of C&H mines.
Photo MTU

I don't know why they call the side tunnels at each level stopes, but that is what they are called.

"Mr. Niemi," Mr. Hakala said. He never calls Papa by his first name out of respect. "That is exactly why we need to join. The union could take complaints like that to the company and get something done about it. The union could make the company men be fair. You told me I had to make up my own mind. Well, I choose to join." He pulled a bunch of coins from his pocket and counted out $2.00.

Mama had been washing the dishes all this time. She had sent my sisters out to play because when the union men came in April there was a big argument. She did not want my sisters to hear if it happened again. When Mr. Hakala handed the union man the money, Mama stiffened. She gave me a look that told me not to say anything about how she had already joined the Women's Auxiliary. I think she was afraid Papa would get so mad he would send Mr. Hakala away.

The man wrote Mr. Hakala's name in a little reddish-brown book and signed it. It looked like a book that shows you have money in a bank. He handed it to Mr. Hakala and said that was his union book to show he was a member. Both men and Mr. Hakala got up and went out the back door. They said something about going to our neighbor across the street to ask him to join.

"Get me more coffee, please, Anna." Mama took the coffee off the stove and filled up Papa's cup. She handed him cream from the icebox.

"Go find your sisters and get on to bed, Emma," Papa told me.

I went through the parlor to the front door. The tiny room just inside the back door, which some families use as a shed, is my brother and Mr. Hakala's bedroom. I go through there only when I have to take the chamber pots to the outhouse. It would not be polite to go through for just anything. I waited a few minutes in the parlor.

Papa drummed his fingers on the table while he waited for Mr. Hakala to come back. He breathed in and out so loudly I could hear him from the parlor. When Mr. Hakala walked in Papa said, "Even though you joined them, you can still stay in our shed with my son."

Wednesday, June 11

———❦———

Another man got killed today down in Hancock while he was using the one-man drill. The paper never even named him. They just said, "A Finn was killed." That made Papa upset. He went on about how they use a Cornish man's name, or an Italian's name, but no names for Finns.

"Maybe it's because they never can spell our names right," Mama said.

"Well, they should learn. We learn to spell theirs," Papa said.

Right then, Mrs. Aittamaa came. She was taking up a collection for the man's wife. "They have four little children," she said. "None old enough to work. What will that poor woman do? Hopefully, the company will let them stay in their house."

Mama looked at Papa, and then at the shelf where she keeps our money until the beginning of a new month when she puts it in the bank. Papa nodded his head. Mama got down the jar but let Papa decide how much to give. Jenni and Katri came running in just then. They froze like snowmen and got very quiet when they saw how everybody was sad. Papa looked at them and at me. His hand began

— 24 —

to shake. "That . . ." he stopped. I think he did not want to say a curse word. "That drill is what they say it is—a widow-maker." He emptied the jar of coins and gave it to Mrs. Aittamaa.

The moon wasn't bright enough to see to write, and since I could not sleep, I stayed awake to think. When Papa looked at me and my sisters with such sad eyes, was he thinking what would happen to us if he got killed?

I was not the only one awake. I could hear Mama and Papa talking in their room. Mama told Papa about Big Annie and the Women's Auxiliary. "It's like an *osu-uskauppa*. We have to help each other like you did tonight. We must stick together and be strong. Please join the union."

"Maybe I will think about it. You know I love you, Anna," I heard Papa say.

———◆———

Thursday, June 12

⎯⎯⊰⧫⊱⎯⎯

Today I decided I should learn more about the problems in the mines. When I had finished my chores, I asked Mama if I could go to the library. We learned about how to find things in the library at school. Besides a lot of books, the library has copies of all the newspapers, even the foreign language ones.

I found some articles in *The Daily Mining Gazette*, which is published in Houghton. I also read a lot in *Työmies*, a Finnish paper whose title means "worker." The *Gazette* mostly says the mining companies are doing their best. They have to compete with the Western mines where they can produce copper more cheaply. The paper points out all the good things the companies give their workers and says how this new one-man drill will be better. The WFM, according to *The Gazette*, is run by a lot of socialists who just want to make trouble in our peaceful communities. I saw the words "outside agitators" a lot.

Työmies says the mining companies are using people like animals. They send all the profits back to Boston to rich company stockholders who know nothing about our area. It seems like only the Cornishmen, or others who came from England, ever get to be mine captains or managers. They say the mine owners get rich on what should belong to the workers. I read a lot of big words like "capitalists" and "impersonal corporate management."

I had to look those words up in the dictionary. "Capitalists" are people who put money into a business and work hard to become rich. I figured out that "impersonal corporate management" means mine captains and office people who do not really care about workers under them. I looked up "socialist", too. It said people who are socialists believe the government should own all the businesses and take care of all the people equally. That sounded a lot like what a co-op does, only with a whole country, not just a group of families. What could be so bad about that?

There was a lot about the one-man drill. The drill they used before had two men running it. *Työmies* said the one-man drill is dangerous because there is only one man. He has to work out of sight of the other men. There is no one to help if something goes wrong and he is hurt. Also, some men might lose their jobs because the new drill uses one man instead of two. There was a lot about safety and the number of men who have been killed since the companies started using it. Using the drill would make it even harder for somebody like my father to work his way up to a better job. Papa and Mr. Hakala talk about that all the time, so I know that's true.

I thought newspapers were supposed to print only the facts, but these papers said the opposite things. Both papers said the other side was wrong and that there was going to be a showdown. I thought I would understand all this better if I read more about it, but I felt more mixed up than ever. My papa doesn't really like the union or C&H, and he has always been honest, so I think I will believe what he says.

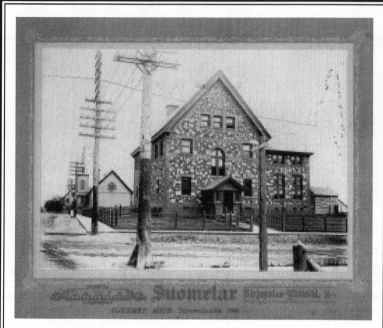

C&H built this public library at the corner of Mine St. and Red Jacket Road, directly across the street from the Pay Office of C&H. The stone walls likely came from the "poor rock" (rock with no copper ore) of a near-by shaft. *Photo MTU-N*

Friday, June 13

They say that when the thirteenth of a month falls on a Friday, it will be bad luck but not today. Mama said it was time for me to learn how to make *juustoa*, oven cheese. I brought in the whole pail from this morning's milking. Mama set an even bigger pot of water on the stove. All the while, Mama explained everything she did. I listened carefully and nodded my head a lot. Mama said to keep feeling the milk and take it off the stove when it was warm, but not hot, to my hand. She added a little salt, sugar, and some rennet to the milk. She buys the rennet from the Finnish store at Pine and 5th Street. She told me it is made from a goat's intestines and it helps the curds and whey separate.

When I took the pot of water off the stove, she set the pail of milk into it and we let it sit. The hot water keeps the milk warm so it makes curds. I went out to weed the garden with Jenni and Katri while it sat. Mama called me in when the milk mixture was ready. I had to scrub my hands and clean under my nails to get all the dirt out. Mama showed me how to stir the milk gently with my hands. As I moved my fingers through the milk, it began to form soft curds. Mama said that was good, and now it had to sit again for a little while longer. She sent me out to the cow shed for more wood for the oven. Then I had to get a clean cheesecloth. It is like thick gauze.

We worked together to ladle the curdled milk into the cheesecloth. The whey drains through the cloth and the curds stay behind. Sometimes we drink the whey, but lately we have been giving it to Mrs. Aittamaa for their pig. We put the curds in Mama's big flat baking pans. A little while later, we poured off more watery whey. By then the oven was hot. We baked the cheese until it was spotted with brown on the top. We turned it over in the pan and put it back in the oven. Mama had me watch it carefully so it did not burn.

Much later, when it was all cool, Mama had me take some of it (and the whey for their pig to eat) to Mrs. Aittamaa. "That's the last of what I owe her for sewing your confirmation dress," Mama said.

———◈———

Saturday, June 14

———◆———

Papa and a lot of the other C&H workers met at the Red Jacket Town Hall today to plan the company picnic. Papa told us at dinner that they will have it at the end of July in the C&H park. My sisters and I liked the sound of that, but Mama said, "We'll see. MacNaughton thinks he can fix everything with a picnic."

"Show some respect in front of the children," Papa said. "Mr. MacNaughton is the general manager. I don't like a lot of what he says and does, but he deserves our respect."

Mama got the coffee pot from the stove and then said, "I respect him as much as I respected that selfish manor owner in Finland. We came here hoping for a better life, but it's no different. The mines are just underground farms. We are still only serfs, and MacNaughton owns the manor."

Everybody—Papa, Mr. Hakala, my brother and sisters, and most of all me—stared at Mama. She never spoke out like this before she started going to the Women's Auxiliary meetings. I wonder what the women do at those meetings to make Mama say such things.

———◆———

Sunday, June 15

O ur preacher talked on and on today about how we must be humble and trust in the Lord. He told everyone to remember what John the Baptist told the soldiers who came to him. They should be satisfied with their wages and treat people decently. Then he read from St. Paul's letter to the Ephesians where he tells slaves to obey their masters, but St. Paul also told the masters to treat their servants well. The preacher told everyone to be patient and the Lord will provide. I heard Mama whisper that she wondered if the mine captains ever listened to those words. I didn't catch it all, but I thought I heard her say, "Maybe C&H bought off the preacher to make us be content." Papa gave her a stern look. Next time I am alone with Mama I will ask her more about all this.

We met Marie and her family as we walked home. I was so glad to see her. We did our best to introduce our families to each other, but since her parents speak mostly French and mine mostly Finnish, there was not a lot to say. Our mamas smiled at each other. My mama cooed at Marie's new baby sister. Marie's mama smiled even more. Our papas nodded politely but did not shake hands.

I whispered to Marie before we went our separate

ways, "Meet me in our meadow place after supper if you can."

When we got back to our house, I asked Mama if I could change and play stick ball for a while before dinner. She told me I could. Right at the back of our garden, the hill drops off sharply, like a little cliff. It is not that high though, maybe twice as tall as I am. There is no house at the bottom, just an empty lot. We gather to play there almost every Sunday. My brother Matti gave me his ball and stick right before he left to go to work for Mr. Lamppa.

We put a pile of gravel for the bases, but they get messed up during the week. The others had the bases scraped back together already when I got there. We played several innings. I struck out the first time I was up to bat, but the next time I hit a good ball and got to first base. The mother of one of the boys called him to dinner, and we all knew it was time to go.

When we sat down to dinner, Papa said, "Only good talk at this table today. Nothing about the mines or work." He looked right at Mr. Hakala and then at Mama.

"Jaako, would you like to go fishing with me this evening?" Mr. Hakala asked. "And you, too, Mr. Niemi?"

"Yes, that would be nice," Papa said.

"The tomato plants are blooming, and the beans, too," Mama said. "Jenni and Katri, you will have to help me weed them tomorrow morning."

Jenni and Katri nodded. There was not much else to say. I looked down. Forks clicking against plates were the only sounds. I looked up and saw that everyone else was looking down. We all seemed to eat quickly.

"A good dinner, Mrs. Niemi," Mr. Hakala said. My father and Jaako agreed. They headed out the door to get their fishing poles from the cow shed.

My sisters and I washed and dried the dishes quickly. Then I was free to go into the meadow and meet Marie.

Marie was not there yet so I made a chain of dandelions while I waited.

"What took you so long?" I asked when she finally came.

"The baby was fussy. I had to take care of my little sisters while Mama fed her."

"Here," I held out the dandelion chain.

"Thank you." Marie smiled and put it around her neck.

We looked at each other, and I knew we were both thinking about how our fathers did not shake hands that morning. I sighed. "I do not think our fathers will ever be friends like we are."

Marie looked at the ground. "My papa says bad things about that union and the people like your papa who join it."

"My papa has not joined. He does not like it much, either. Maybe it will help if you tell him that."

"I don't think so, Emma. I am afraid. What if the men go on strike? My papa will never strike. He said so, very loudly at dinner. He said Big Annie is a troublemaker. He told Mama` to shun her if she sees her on the street." Marie started to cry. "Papa told me he does not want me to see you any more. I had to sneak over here. If he catches me . . . "

I bit my lip so I would not start crying, too. I put my arms around Marie. "It will be all right. Obey your

Papa. Maybe all this talk about a strike will go away soon. We will know we are still friends in our hearts. Nobody can stop that. It will be our secret until school starts again."

I gave Marie my handkerchief to dry her tears. I held a dandelion under her chin. "See, the sun is shining on your chin, so smile."

Marie sniffed and we both stood up, and we hugged each other. Marie started crying all over again. I could not stop myself then. The tears rolled down my cheeks.

Wednesday, June 18

M ama gave me her shopping list and money to day. This is the first time she has trusted me to do any shopping by myself. I think I know how young birds must feel when they fly out of the nest for the first time, afraid and excited all at once. I walked up to Pine Street to the Finnish store. While I was there, I saw some of the students from the class ahead of me cleaning out the shop owner's storeroom. They finished right before I paid for Mama's groceries. The owner let them choose a hand full of hard candy for their pay. I thought I should try doing that, too.

After I took Mama's groceries home, she said I was free to do as I pleased. I went back but the others had already been to all the shops on Pine Street ahead of me. Nobody needed any more work done. I will try again tomorrow in a different part of town.

On my way home the second time, I walked by the Opera House. I stopped and watched a fine lady dressed in a pink summer gown. She wore white gloves that went up past her elbow. The upper part of her arm showed just a little between the top of the glove and the lace on the sleeve of her gown. She put down her parasol and walked up to the box office. I heard her ask to buy tickets to the next performance. Then I heard beautiful music start, stop, and start again. I guess the singers and musicians were practicing inside. How I wish I could go in there, but I know I cannot. It costs much more than flicker pictures at the Bijou.

As I turned to go, there was a rumbling sound and the street shook a little. Everyone in the street stopped. People came out of shops and stood still. The mine levels and stopes run under the town of Red Jacket. The streets always rumble a bit when they are blasting, but this was not the usual time of day for that. Had there been an accident?

People around me whispered. After a minute or so, when no sirens went off, people went back to whatever they were doing. For those people it was just another one of those rumblings that come and go, but I was thinking about Papa. I let out a big breath I didn't realize I had been holding.

Sometimes when Mama takes all of us shopping, we walk by all the fancy dress shops, look in the windows and dream. I didn't feel like doing that today. I sighed and walked along Sixth Street which is paved with bricks. I thought about Marie as I passed near her church and turned to go toward Swedetown. Somehow, our dirt road seemed dustier than usual.

⋙◆⋘

Friday, June 20

I walked over to Laurium after I finished my chores to-day. I thought maybe the shops there might have some back rooms in need of cleaning. Some shopkeepers said they had no work for a girl like me. Then I got lucky in Mr. Edwards' grocery. He said there were bushels of potatoes that needed to be sorted and the rotten ones tossed out. I went to work on it, even though the smell was bad.

I put the really rotten ones in one pile, the good ones in another and those that had some rotten parts and some good parts in a third pile. Mr. Edwards had me put the good ones in a new bushel basket and the rotten ones in the trash bin.

"What about these?" I asked pointing to the half good ones.

"I can't sell them. You may have them, if you want them. Come and choose some candy for your work."

"Thank you, Sir," I said. I chose *vanhapojan kääntiä*, peppermint candies, my family's favorite. "May I come back and help you again sometime?"

Before Mr. Edwards could answer, a woman came into the shop with a list. She tried to speak English but nothing came out right. I wasn't sure if she was Finnish, Croatian, or something else, but I asked in Finnish if I could help her. She smiled and told me how she worked for a family on Pewabic Street and her mistress wanted her to shop at this store. I took her list and helped her find each thing. When it was all on the counter, and the woman got out the money her mistress had given her, Mr. Edwards smiled at me.

"Thank you for all your help. What's your name, young lady?"

"Emma Niemi," I said.

"Well, Miss Niemi, you are welcome to come back here any time." He handed me another bunch of peppermints.

"Thank you, Sir." I felt as proud as I did the day I won the essay contest.

The peppermints made my dress pocket bulge. The box of half good potatoes seemed light on the long walk home. Jenni and I spent the late afternoon cutting off the good parts and peeling them for a big pot of mashed potatoes for supper. When I pulled the peppermints out of my pocket and passed them around for dessert, everybody shouted, "*Vanhapojan Kääntiä!*"

Thursday, June 26

Two days ago, everything started out so fine. It was warm and sunny. I finished all my chores and decided to go to Mr. Edwards' store again. Then everything went so wrong that I could not make myself write about it until today.

I was about halfway down the Swedetown road and not far from Papa's mine shaft. The ground shook and rumbled something awful! Sirens blared. A lot of people started running toward the shaft. I ran back up the road and almost plowed into Mama as she ran toward the mine shaft.

"Go stay with your sisters. I'll . . . find out . . . what the trouble is." I had never heard Mama's voice shake like that. Her face looked as white as clean sheets on a line. I bit my lip and ran home.

"What's wrong? What's wrong?" Jenni and Katri cried. "Mama ran off so fast. Are Papa and Jaako all right?"

I put my arms around my sisters and tried to be brave for them. "I don't know," I said. "Mama will come back and tell us soon."

But it wasn't soon. We tried to keep busy. Jenni dusted the parlor. Katri weeded around the tomatoes again. But all we could think about was the mine. Was there a big explosion? Was there a fire in the mine? Was our Papa dead? Or our brother Jaako?

Finally, we sat down on the front steps to wait. All up and down the street, women and children were sitting the same way. I told Jenni and Katri every story Papa had ever told me. They were not really listening. We sat, arms around each other, and stared at the ground.

A loud wailing reached our ears. A crowd of women and a few men came slowly up the hill along with a cart. I felt as if I were frozen to the steps. I could not move. The cart came closer and closer to our house, but I could not see Mama or Papa.

Katri started to cry. Then Jenni yelled, "Mama! Papa! Look, Emma, there they are! And Jaako, too!"

Jenni and Katri jumped up and ran down the hill, but I could not move.

The crowd and the cart stopped in front of our steps. Jenni and Katri were hugging Mama and Papa. Both Mama and Papa had tears in their eyes.

"Emma!" Papa cried, "it's all right." Papa walked over to me and put his hands on my shoulders. Tears streamed down my face. He pushed my hair back from my face and kissed my forehead. "Please take your sisters over to Mrs. Aittamaa's," he said. "Your mama and I have something we have to do."

It was Mr. Hakala's body in the cart. He was so covered with dirt I hardly knew him. Jaako stood between the cart and my sisters so they could not see.

Mrs. Aittamaa welcomed my sisters and me. We sat down and said a prayer of thanks for Papa, Jaako and Mr.

Aittamaa, and asked God to take Mr. Hakala into heaven. Then Mrs. Aittamaa got out her ice cream maker. She said, "A cold treat will help ease your minds." She poured milk, eggs, sugar and vanilla into the inner tin and put on the lid. Next she put the tin in the bucket. She handed me the ice pick to chip ice from the block in the icebox. Jenni and Katri packed the ice around the tin. Mrs. Aittamaa put salt on the ice and attached the crank handle.

We turned the crank round and round until the salt melted the ice and the milk froze in the tin. By the time we had worn out our arms turning the crank, the ice cream was ready. Mama came to get us just as we finished eating it.

She and Papa had washed Mr. Hakala's body and dressed him in his church suit. He was laid out in a coffin in the parlor. All evening people came and went, talking softly to Mama and Papa and putting coins in a can. Papa kept telling people what a good man Mr. Hakala was, and how he had finally saved up enough money to bring his wife and child to America. Papa will have the bank send his widow the money and maybe it will help them live in Finland a little longer.

I listened as some of the men talked about the accident. Papa and Mr. Hakala were down at the end of the stope near where the miners were drilling holes for the next blast. The drill must have hit a crack or an air pocket: nobody knew quite what happened. A huge piece of rock on the hanging wall above them fell. Mr. Hakala was crushed beneath it, not two feet from where Papa and Jaako were lifting rock into the tram car.

The lump in my throat felt like a whole apple. I

thank God I still have my papa, but I almost feel guilty in my thankfulness, because Mr. Hakala's wife and child have no one to support them now.

The "hanging wall" or ceiling could collapse at any time, even in a well-timbered mine. The human cost of copper has been estimated at one man dead, ten serious injuries and as many as 100 minor injuries per week. *Photo MTU*

The next day we buried Mr. Hakala. I will never forget how I choked on the words of one of the hymns:

Blest be the tie that binds our hearts in Christian love.
The fellowship of kindred hearts is like to that above.
We share our mutual woes. Our mutual burdens bear.
And often for each other flows a sympathizing tear. . . .

This morning at breakfast, Papa slammed his fist

on the table. "After pushing that darn tram car ten hours a day for nearly thirteen years, I still don't have enough money to buy land. Anna, you are right. *Minä olen vain vuokralainen ja MacNaughton omistaa kartanon.*" (I am still just a tenant and MacNaughton owns the manor.)

He got up and walked out of the kitchen. On his way out he said, "After I pick up the rest of Mr. Hakala's pay and take all the money to the bank, I am going down to the WFM Hall and I will join."

—◆—

Tomorrow is our church summer picnic at the lakeshore. Mama and I spent most of the day baking bread and making *juustoa* to share. I am glad that was all we had to make. Other families will bring food to share, too. We will play games and run races. Lake Superior might still be very cold, so we may not want to swim but maybe I will wade a little. If I am lucky, I might find an agate among the pebbles and sand. If I do, I will put it on Mr. Hakala's grave.

Last Sunday, most of the girls and boys in my confirmation class told me their families would be going to the picnic. This will be the first time we can be together in a fun way. All through the year as we studied for our confirmation, we had to be very serious. There was always prayer and quiet, or reciting memorized Bible verses, or pages from Luther's Catechism but never any laughter. Even the week after Easter, when we were confirmed, it was all prayer and praise to God at the dinner. Of course we smiled at each other, but any hint of a giggle would have made our teacher cross.

Back then, I could think of nothing but how we girls could be as silly as we wanted at the picnic. Now, I cannot stop thinking about the empty place at our table. I don't want to be silly anymore.

Papa always comes home a little earlier on Saturdays. We headed for Palosaari's Sauna, as is our habit. Mama, my sisters and I go to the women's side, and the men go to their side. I grabbed six towels from the linen shelf before I realized I only needed five. I got that lump in my throat again as I put one back. I bit my lip so I would not cry again. When we were in the hot sauna room, sitting on *lautat*, cedar benches set like bleachers, I asked Mama if she could put more water on the hot rocks to make more *löylyä*, steam. That way I could let my tears out slowly, and others would think it was only sweat.

I think Mama knew though. She gently swatted my back with a birch bough soaked in hot water we call a *vihta*, and rubbed my shoulders and neck. Between Mama's rubbing and swatting, I felt tingly and relaxed all over.

On the walk home, Papa started talking about the two men from Swedetown who play on the Calumet area baseball team. They played against the Lake Linden team last week. Calumet won four to one. If we keep playing like this, our team may go on to win for the region. All of us in Swedetown hope our men will make us proud.

Papa said, "We need to get on with our lives. That's what Juhani would want us to do. We will all go and watch the game after supper."

Y ou and the children go on home," Papa said right after church this morning. "Get everything ready for the picnic. We will leave as soon as I get back from the WFM meeting." It is hard to get used to the change in Papa since Mr. Hakala died. Two weeks ago, he would not let us talk about the WFM. Now he talks about it all the time.

Jaako wanted to go with Papa since they both joined the union. Papa told him to help get everything ready. Mr. and Mrs. Aittamaa have a horse and cart, so we will ride with them out to the picnic ground.

We had everything in the cart when Papa and Mr. Aittamaa got back. The men rode on the wagon bench. Mama, Mrs. Aittamaa, Jenni, Katri and I rode in the bed of the cart along with the picnic basket and blankets.

We listened as Papa told Jaako about the meeting. "The WFM leaders in Denver are glad to see so many men join now," Papa said. "They think we should wait until next spring before we try to strike. The leaders say the union's treasury is too low to fight a big company like C&H. Summer is wearing on, and we need all the good weather months to fight the company."

"So what will we do?" Jaako asked.

"You know how the miners usually treat us trammers like dirt? Well, even I was surprised at how they listen to us now. Nobody likes the one-man drill. Big Annie pulled all the men together." Papa laughed. "Italians, Finns, Slavs, Poles, Croatians, even a few of those uppity Cornish miners who think they are better than everybody else because they have been here the longest, don't like C&H. We may not trust each other very much, but we are all against the company."

Papa turned around, "You hear that, Anna? You were right again."

Mama and I smiled at each other.

The five local union groups have combined into District Union No. 16. Papa went on to say that there would be a referendum from July 1 until July 12. WFM members from Mohawk, Calumet, Hancock and on down to South Range will vote on two things: first, whether or not the union should ask for a meeting with company managers from C&H, Quincy Mining Co., and the other smaller companies, and second, whether they should strike if the company managers will not meet with them and listen to what the men want.

"What's a referendum?" Jaako asked.

"It is sort of like an election. We will vote what we feel, but things could still change," Papa said. "It will let our local union officials know how everybody feels. Then they can plan best how to go to the company. There will be another vote later."

"How will you vote, Papa?" Jaako asked.

"I am not sure. I am against what the company is doing these days, but I do not want those hot-head socialists down in Hancock to jump into a strike without thinking carefully."

"What about you, Mr. Aittamaa?"

"I think your Papa may be right," Mr. Aittamaa said.

By this time, we were almost to the picnic ground on Lake Superior. Katri began to hang over the side of the wagon. She pointed to the lake as we came out of the trees. "Look! It is so beautiful today."

It truly was. The clear sky and light wind made the lake a huge cape of royal blue with white lace where the waves broke on the shore. We could see some people wading. A few children had jumped right in for a cold swim.

I ran off to find my friends while Mama, Papa and the others took our food to the big table and laid out our blankets. I took off my shoes and wiggled my toes in a patch of warm sand on the pebble beach. Lempi, who always sat next to me during confirmation class, ran up to me. We raced down the shore until we could not run any more.

All tired out, we sat down. "I was waiting for you," Lempi said. "Let's look for agates."

I looked and looked, but I did not find any.

We heard some of the men whistle. It was time to come together to say a blessing over all the food and eat. When I could not eat another bite, I lay back on our family's blanket and looked at the sky.

Lempi came and sat down beside me. "I found an agate," she said. "Here. You may have it."

"Thank you," I said. "I was hoping to find one to

put on Mr. Hakala's grave." The lump in my throat was smaller this time, making it easier to swallow. Even though I miss Mr. Hakala and I cannot see Marie for a while, I still have Lempi for a friend.

Monday, June 30

L ast night after we came home from the picnic, I overheard Mama and Papa talking. They were try-ing to decide if we should take in another man to board with us. They never charged Mr. Hakala any money, but now Papa said they should ask for a few dol-lars a month room and board. The money would go into the bank toward our farm.

I could barely hear Mama's reply, "Juhani was like a son to us. The rent would be good, but if there is a strike, that man would not have money to pay. We would have another mouth to feed with no money coming in. Besides, Matti will be home in the fall."

Their voices got softer, but I think they decided to wait a few months and see how things go between the union and C&H. I am glad we will not have anyone new for awhile.

Independence Day is my favorite holiday of the whole year! We all walked up to Fifth Street to watch the big parade. Thousands of people lined the streets. It was hard to find a place to stand and watch.

Street scene on Fifth Street in Red Jacket (Calumet). Many more people would have gathered for a Fourth of July Parade. *Photo MTU*

"You girls hold onto each other," Mama said. "If you go off on your own, just walk on over to the park after the parade. We will find you there."

The C&H band marched behind a group of Veterans from the Spanish-American war who carried United States and Michigan flags. Behind them came real automobiles! Very old men, veterans of the Civil War rode in them. They seemed proud to wear their uniforms. The village councilmen rode in fancy carriages all decorated in red, white and blue streamers. My family cheered extra loud when the Finnish Humu band marched by. Lots of businesses had horse-drawn wagons all decorated with streamers and signs for their stores. There was a man on stilts dressed like Uncle Sam, and clowns, and so many others. Firecrackers popped and snapped all around us. Fire trucks, with their bells clanging, were loaded with children and decorated with flowers and streamers. They were the end of the parade.

Jaako gave Jenni, Katri and me a few pennies to buy sparklers. Neither he, nor Papa, would let us buy any firecrackers. Mama says they are much too dangerous. Mama went on and on about how every year several people get burned when the firecrackers go off too soon. Tomorrow's paper will probably be full of such stories about this year's celebration.

In the park, village council members and some from the township made speeches about how wonderful our country is and how blessed we are to live in this great land. Then there were games and races. Jenni and I entered the three-legged race, but Jenni tripped at the start. We had a hard time getting our outer legs in rhythm. Because Jenni is shorter than I am, our inner legs, tied at our knees and ankles, would not work together. We came in last. Jaako laughed and said it was good that we tried.

He entered the "Miller and Sweep" contest. Jaako

had the miller's sack of flour and stood in one barrel. Another young man, the sweep, stood in a barrel a few feet away. His sack was full of ashes. They bopped each other with the sacks until Jaako knocked the other man over. Everyone laughed as Jaako claimed his prize—a ticket for a free beer at one of the taverns. Both men were covered with flour and soot. Papa took the ticket and gave it back to the other man because we do not believe in drinking beer, wine, or anything like that.

The other man looked at all of us and took some coins from his pocket. "Here is the money I would have spent on a beer. Buy the children some ice cream," he said.

The games and races went on most of the afternoon. Papa bought us all some Cracker Jack. We watched more games, listened to the bands play for a while and then began the walk home. After supper, most of the people in Swedetown sat at the edge of our hill to watch the fireworks. Mama helped us light our sparklers. We all wrote our names in the air with light. Katri still blocks her ears because she says the booming and popping noises frighten her. I think the exploding sounds are to remind us of those who had to die for our freedom. The bursts of color against the stars are the glory they have now.

I had saved one last sparkler for after the fireworks. When everything else was dark, I waved it in the air. Inside my mind I said, "This one is for you, Mr. Hakala." This time I didn't have any lump in my throat. It was a very good feeling.

Wednesday, July 9

Papa and Jaako went to an important union meeting tonight. When they came home, Papa called all the family together around the kitchen table. His face looked so strange—like he was trying to smile and frown at the same time.

"The referendum is not complete yet, but so far 98% of the members approve a strike if the owners will not meet with us," Papa said. "WFM officials in Denver want us to wait until they meet on the 14th before we send our letters to the owners." He sighed, "The Hancock local already passed a resolution and sent it to us and the other locals. They want the District Board to meet right away, even before the referendum is finished. They called for the owners to tell us by July 21 whether they will meet with us or not."

Jaako added, "Mr. Mahoney, one of the WFM officials, wants us to wait until he can be here to help."

"Yes," Papa said, "and Hancock won't wait. Nobody thinks a strike will last long, but I think we need to make plans for our family."

Mama had made coffee and she poured cups for Papa, Jaako and herself while she waited for Papa to tell us what to do. I did not know what to think. I kept staring at a crack in the table.

Papa took a sip before speaking. "Everybody in this family can help in some way. I will be the one to march in the picket line. Jaako, I want you to use every day we don't work to fish and set rabbit snares in the woods. We will build a little smokehouse to cure and dry the fish. Try to catch a pair of rabbits. We will build a hutch for them and have fresh meat through the fall. You girls will keep the rabbits fed with fresh clover from the field. Emma, I want you to teach Jenni all your chores. See if you can work a little more for that grocer in Laurium or anybody else. Ask if they can give you flour or sugar instead of candy for your pay."

What a relief. My part will be easy. I told Papa I would do that.

Papa went on, "All three of you, pick every wild berry you can find, and then find and pick some more. Anna, you can use a little of the land money to buy more jars for canning. I will write a letter to Matti. Maybe he can find some extra work in that lumber mill down in Lake Linden when Mr. Lamppa does not need him in the fall—if the strike is not over by then."

Mama said, "With smoked fish, rabbits, and all the berries and vegetables I will put up, our cow, the potatoes and onions Matti will earn, we will have most of the food we need. What about rent money?"

"The union is supposed to help us with the strike fund to replace some of our pay," Papa said. "With Jaako and I both members, we each get a little. I think that will cover the rent."

Nobody needed to say that we would not plan to buy anything we didn't really need. Jaako said he would also spend time in the woods getting firewood, so we wouldn't have to buy as much coal. Mama got up and put out one of the kerosene lamps, saying one would do.

Papa drank the last of his coffee and said we would pray together. "God and Father of us all," he prayed, "thank you for my family, for children willing to work and help. Grant us extra *sisu* in the weeks to come. If there has to be a strike, Lord, let it be short. Amen."

We said goodnight to each other. When I climbed the stairs, I think my face was like Papa's had been—both happy and angry. There won't be anymore ice cream or Cracker Jack or any treats at all. I thought about what Marie said last winter about *Mardi Gras* and Lent. Her whole family gives up sweets, meat on Wednesdays and Fridays and all sorts of other stuff. I didn't think about it then, but I guess the 4th of July was our *Mardi Gras*. I was glad there was a little twilight left to write by. From now on, I will not be able to use an oil lamp. I wonder how long this "Lent" will last.

———◆———

Friday, July 11

—◆—

Mr. Edwards was happy to see me this morning. I sorted out a barrel of apples from last fall and helped two Finnish-speaking women who came into the store. He let me keep the half-good apples and gave me a half a pound of sugar and a bit of cinnamon—all that Mama needs to make applesauce.

Mr. Edwards did something that really surprised me. He asked if I could come every Friday. He got a piece of paper and a pencil and asked if I would make a sign for his window saying: "*Soumea puhutaan,* Finnish is spoken here: Fridays from 1 to 4 PM."

The box full of apples and sugar was heavy, but I started the long walk home on dancing feet. As I passed by the library on Red Jacket Road, who should be coming out of the library but Marie!

"Emma!" she cried out. "I am so glad to see you!"

I set down the box and hugged her. She said nobody from her family would know, so we sat down right there in the shade of a big tree. I told her about Mr. Hakala and how Papa had joined the WFM.

"I am so sorry to hear that," she said. "My father is still very much against all of this."

Her father works in the carpentry shop, not down underground. The pay is just as low, but it is much safer. We think maybe that is why our parents feel so differently about the union.

"This is very odd," I said. "Here we are, sitting in front of the library that C&H built. We look across the street at the company office buildings. Our fathers hate each other, but we are best friends."

"Maybe when we grow up, we will teach our children that we can all be friends."

"I promise that. Now, let's talk about good things," I said.

Marie told me that her family had gone to a dance at Electric Park two Saturdays ago. "Our whole family, even Mamá with baby Bridgett, got on the trolley. I carried our picnic basket. Oh, Emma, you should see how beautiful it is when they turn on all the lights!"

The trolley company built Electric Park about half of the way between Red Jacket and Hancock, not far from Boston Location. Our family went there once last summer on a Sunday afternoon. Papa will go on Sunday because they do not serve beer or other drinks like that then. There are swings, teeter-totters and sandboxes for children to play. There is a big dance hall where a band plays almost every Saturday.

Marie went on, "While Mamá took care of Bridgett, Papá taught me how to dance. He said he wants me to learn now, so when I am older and boys ask me to dance, I will already know what to do." She said it was very late when they got home. They slept later than usual and went to the second service, which she called mass, instead of the early one they usually attend. I had not realized that Catholics can go to church at different times. We have only one service at our church.

I told Marie about how I will be working over in Laurium. "I will be walking by here every Friday right about this time. We could see each other again this way," I said.

"And I will have to return these books! That will be just right."

We talked a little more as we walked up Red Jacket Road and past St. Anne's church. After another block, she went her way and I turned to take the road to Swedetown. Even though I was tired, and it had been a very long walk, and the apples were heavy, I felt even more like dancing.

———◦◦———

Whan Papa got home from work today, he handed me a letter that had been put in his pay envelope. "Jaako could only figure out about half of this," he said. "Please read it for us, Emma."

Papa knows a little English when someone speaks to him, but he doesn't read it at all. Jaako knows more, but he only stayed in school a few years before he started work to help the family.

The letter was from the company management. It said that beginning August 1, any employee who is hurt while working will be paid $1 per day while he gets better. The money will come from an aid fund C&H will set up. Men will start getting this money on the sixth day after their accident. Michigan passed a law earlier this year to make companies help their workers, so C&H had to do something.

"A dollar a day is not very much," Mama said.

"So the rumors going around were true. Tossing out such a bone will only make some of the men angrier. Someone said that MacNaughton had Sheriff Cruse deputize some 250 company men to guard the mines if we strike. Up to Mohawk and down to South Range, there are more men in the union than not. Here in Calumet, not as many men agree with the WFM, but it is here that union leaders want to make the strongest stand. C&H is the biggest and most powerful of all the mining companies. Getting them to shut down will be a big victory for everyone."

"Big Annie and many of the other women believe we can win," Mama said.

"There are a lot of the single men. They drink too much and don't go to church. They got hot heads."

Mama shook her head and said nothing more. With all that in mind, we left for Palosaari's Sauna. All the way, I wished all the strike talk would just go away.

<hr />

Wednesday, July 16

O ur cow Daisy does not like Jenni as much as she likes me. The first time Jenni tried to milk her, she kicked Jenni right off the stool. Luckily, Jenni was not hurt. I took over and had Jenni sit next to me. Then Jenni and I each used one hand to trick her. Jenni finally did finish milking her. Mama said we should do that for a few days to get Daisy used to Jenni.

Katri is getting really good at helping Mama in the garden. Her little fingers pull weeds faster than anybody I know. Mama sent us all out into the meadow with our berry buckets this afternoon. We came home with our buckets full of wild raspberries. Mama said we should go every day now. Of course, we were not the only ones. There must have been twenty children just like us out there picking.

"Go earlier tomorrow," Mama said. "Try to get there before there are so many others. Emma, when your bucket is full, leave it with your sisters. Go and wander about. See if you can find other patches a bit farther away that others have not found."

Papa came home with more bad news. Another family of seven children down in South Range is without a father.

"Is it anybody we know?" Mama asked. "Should we . . ."

"No, we don't need to give anything. There will be other neighbors this time."

We told Papa about all the berries we picked. He said that was good, but then he added, "I'm sorry, but we will not take the 3-H Special to Freda Park this Sunday. I know I promised that earlier this summer, but things are different now."

I saw Katri bite her lip just before I looked at the floor. The rest of dinner was very quiet again.

I filled the silence with my memories of last summer's trip. It was such a wonderful adventure! The Copper Range Railroad ran its 3-H special several times every Sunday. We got on the train at the Calumet station. It made stops to take on more people in Hubbell, Hancock and Houghton before winding its way to the shore of Lake Superior to Freda. Even though we are only about six miles from the lakeshore here, it was exciting to travel farther down the Keweenaw Peninsula, almost thirty miles in all. There were so many people, streets, houses and stores, especially in Hancock and Houghton, and beautiful fields and woods along the way to Freda.

Papa and Mama saw much of the world when they left Finland to come here. Jaako remembers the journey. He told me once how wonderful it was to see the Statue of Liberty when they reached New York City. Matti does not remember much of that, but he does travel down to Lake Linden and out into the Trap Rock Valley to work for Mr. Lamppa. That is not very far, but it is someplace different. Last summer's trip to Freda Park was the only place I have ever been besides our church picnic each year and where my own two feet take me.

Maybe, when I will go into the library on my way home from Mr. Edwards' store this Friday, I will check out a book on some far away country and go there in my mind. But for now, I must only dream. The twilight is nearly gone, and I cannot see to write any more. I must sleep so I can get up early to stain my fingers raspberry red again tomorrow.

———❦———

Thursday, July 17

The paper today told all about how the Upper Peninsula Firemen's Association will come next week for their tournament. There is a tournament like this every year, but this is the first year I can remember them coming here. They are going to string more than 2000 lights all along Fifth, Sixth, Scott and several other streets to welcome them.

We will have picked about all the raspberries there are by then and the blueberries are not yet ripe. Maybe we will all go and watch the tournament since it is free. The paper says there will be contests between the firemen of each town. They will show how fast they can unroll hoses. There will be a barrel on a rope high in the air. Two teams will spray water from the fire hoses at it and try to push it along the rope, back and forth until one team gets it across the other team's line. The men working the pumps must try to get the most pressure into their hose to win. All of it will show the firemen's strength and skills to put out fires. It sounds like it would be as much fun to watch as the games on the 4th of July. The paper said that none of these men are paid to fight fires. They live in the towns close to the fire stations. When there is an alarm, they leave their jobs or businesses to go and put out the fire. I hope I get to go to the tournament even though I have so much work to do.

Friday, July 18

I checked out a book at the library today. I got to see Marie, too, but that tiny bit of good feeling blew away like dust in the street. Papa and Jaako came home from another WFM meeting. Mr. Hietala and the other local WFM leaders have gone ahead on their own and mailed the demands to the companies without waiting for WFM leaders in Denver to say they should.

Mr. Hietala gave the companies until July 21 to say if they will meet with the union. Papa said it does not sound like anything will stop a strike now. Everywhere I go, people are either talking about it with loud, angry voices, or in whispers, as if they are planning something bad. Mama and Papa, Mr. and Mrs. Aittamaa, and so many others around here always have worry lines on their faces.

I want to get it over with. Maybe it will be better after our men and the companies say what they have to say. Whenever I get angry at Jenni or Katri, I cannot listen to them. If I let it out and yell at them, I feel bad afterward. I say I am sorry and listen to them. Then we all get along again.

Maybe the meeting between the company managers

and the union will be like my arguments with my sisters. They will yell at each other and then listen. The mine managers and the workers are grown-ups, aren't they?

———◆———

———❖———

Papa hung his head and told us this evening that none of the mining companies made any reply to their letters. Quincy Mining Company over in Hancock returned theirs unopened. WFM members voted to strike beginning tomorrow. I guess there won't even be any yelling. Why won't they even try to listen?

"I will go over to the Palestra in Laurium early tomorrow morning," Papa said. "The rest of you go ahead and enjoy the Firemen's Tournament."

Jenni and I smiled. Katri yelled, "Yea!"

Papa smiled, too, but later his shoulders sagged as he walked up the steps to go to bed. We all followed him. I sat here by the window wanting to write more, but I could not. I am afraid.

———❖———

Thursday, July 24

I was too shocked last night to write. What happened yesterday was a thousand, no, a million times, worse than any fight I ever had with my sisters. Mama, Jaako, Jenni, Katri and I went to watch the Firemen's Tournament, as Papa had said we should. A carnival had been set up on the park grounds, too. We had no money to spend there, so we went around it to watch the hose contests and listen to the bands play. One team, I do not remember which, was really good. We watched them beat several others moving the barrel along the rope with the spray of water. We all cheered for the winners.

All of a sudden, we heard a roaring of shouts and cries from the far side of the park closer to Mine Street where many of the shafts are located. Jaako said he would go see what the trouble was. He came running back a few minutes later.

"Mama, you better take the girls home. There is a riot going on at the shafts. Don't go near there! Take Oak Street over to Sixth and then on to home."

"What about you?" Mama asked. "If you do not see your Papa, get away from the trouble."

"I will," Jaako said and hurried away.

Mama took Jenni by one hand and Katri by the other. "Stay close to us," she told me.

We hurried across the park to Fourth Street. I looked down toward where Jaako went. People were running everywhere. I saw some men running up Red Jacket Road carrying sticks and shovels, swinging them in the air. I almost got lost from Mama as the crowd of people from the park ran all around us.

As we got away from the park, there were fewer people. Mama hurried us along Oak Street all the way to Eighth where we turned and walked back to where we could take our road home. At each corner, we could see the mob moving along Sixth, off toward Tamarack Location. Mama did not let us slow down until we were at the bottom of Swedetown hill.

Many neighbors were out and about. Everyone had a different story. I only caught bits and pieces.

"Lots of men got beaten."

"An old man was taken to the hospital."

"Deputies had clubs, hit our men."

"Rocks flying everywhere."

"Some men said they'd kill anybody carrying a dinner pail tomorrow."

Jenni and Katri were crying by the time we reached our front steps. We sat down and Mama hugged us. She tried to smile, but her voice shook as she said to me, "Emma, will you get us all some water, and maybe some bread and *juustoa*? We will have a little snack while we wait for Papa and Jaako."

I nodded and went in. I almost tripped over my feet.

It felt like I was numb and dizzy, and I could not think right at all. My hands shook as I picked up the water jug and the bread. I thought I would drop the jug.

"Mama!" I shouted.

Mama came in the door as I burst into tears. She took the jug, set it on the table, and helped me into a kitchen chair. I grabbed her around the middle like I used to when I was a little girl and buried my face in her chest.

"It is all right, Emma," Mama said and stroked my hair. "Do not worry now. I will take the jug outside."

I sat there shaking while Mama picked up some mugs and took the jug and the bread to Jenni and Katri. When she came back in, I felt better. I carried the *juustoa* out on a plate.

It was way past eight in the evening when we saw Jaako guiding Papa up the street. Papa had his hand on his head. Jenni and Katri started crying all over again. We stood aside for Papa and Jaako and then followed them into the kitchen.

All of us crowded around the table while Mama heated some water to wash Papa's face.

"What in the name of heaven happened?" Mama asked.

Papa sipped some water from a mug before he told us his story. He was at the Palestra, a very big auditorium over in Laurium. The WFM members had been talking there on and off all day. In the afternoon, they had a meeting and listened to the union leaders. Everyone was peaceful and orderly as they left. They marched up Depot Street to Calumet Avenue and then turned toward Red

Jacket. Papa said he could not figure out quite what happened. One minute they were calm with their march and the next, many of the men seemed to explode.

A building similar to The Palestra in Laurium. Archivists think this may actually be the Glaciadome in Mohawk. The building is now in Marquette. *Photo MTU-N*

"Like how the clouds build up and build up," he said, "then all of a sudden, BANG! Lightning strikes. Many strikers swarmed over the mine properties like hornets when you break their nest!" Papa said. He told how the deputies started swinging their night sticks. The men got more and more angry, shouting and out of control.

Papa stopped for a minute while Mama put a hot, wet cloth on his forehead. "I'm all right," he said, but Mama insisted she had to clean the wound carefully.

Papa told us he tried to get away from the mob, but it was like he was caught up in a rushing current of water. The crowd pushed him along to the next shaft. He worked his way to the edge of the crowd near shaft number five, and then a flying rock hit him in the head. He fell and barely rolled out of the way before he would have been trampled. The crowd moved on to the next shaft. Papa stayed where he was until Jaako found him and helped him up.

"It was all crazy," he said.

Mama finished cleaning Papa's forehead and we all headed upstairs. I bit my lip until I was sure Jenni and Katri were asleep. I thought about all Papa said about lightning and hornets and made my pillow all soggy with tears.

———◆———

Friday, July 25

O h, it is such a horrible mess. I think all the world has gone crazy. More people got hurt the second day of the strike. Some strikers attacked a group of men who wanted to go to work. Sometime during the first night, Sheriff Cruse telegraphed Governor Ferris. The newspaper reported that Sheriff Cruse said the riot was out of control and that it was an assault on private property. His deputies could not cope with it. They are sending in the Michigan National Guard! By yesterday morning, the governors of Illinois, Wisconsin and Indiana also ordered their National Guard reserves to board trains for the Keweenaw Peninsula, which is our special part of Michigan's Upper Peninsula. Somebody threatened to kill Sheriff Cruse for ordering up the National Guard. Another rumor said that Mr. MacNaughton and his family had to leave their house and stay where nobody can find them. They say he has someone to guard him all the time, but the mines are shut down now.

Things quieted down today. The mine managers closed all underground and surface work except for operating the pumps. Even the strikers know that the pumps must keep running or the lower levels of the mines will fill with water. The carnival packed up and left. I do not remember seeing in the paper which team finally won the firemen's tournament.

Strikers marching with a band in front. Many union men played musical instruments. *Photo MTU-N*

The men had a big parade starting at the Italian Hall and it was mostly peaceful. All of the women and children stood along the way cheering for them. I felt proud when Papa and Jaako walked by. They both looked straight ahead and were as quiet as they are in church. Big Annie carried the biggest American flag I ever saw on a ten-foot pole at the head of the parade. She was all dressed up like women do for church in her high button shoes and a broad-brimmed hat with a feather in it. All the union officials had on their best suits. Big Annie said that we must show them we mean business—that this is not a feudal system and we are not serfs. I heard later there were a few fist fights along the edges of the parade, but we did not see any.

The special trains with the soldiers started rattling by our hill late this afternoon. We walked down to the bridge over the railroad tracks to watch. When Papa came home to supper, he told us that the park all around the Armory looked like a big military camp. Lots of men were saying that Governor Ferris answered the demands of the working men with bayonets. Papa also said that the company managers were actually glad there was a riot.

"It makes them look like the victims," Papa said, "and us union men look like the bad guys." He shook his head in disgust. "This will not get the other miners and surface workers to join us."

"Papa," I said, "I saw some reporters who were not from around here talking to Big Annie and they seemed to like her. Why do the newspapers say the strikers are all bad?"

"I heard the mine managers give a lot of money to the local elected officials when they run for office. Store owners pay for a lot of advertising in the papers. Maybe the papers are afraid they will lose that money if they support us. I heard some say most of the businesses support the mine managers because their stores are built on company land."

We were quiet for awhile. Papa said we must follow our plan. Jenni, Katri and I should go looking for blueberries. Jaako will check the rabbit traps and spend the day fishing. I did not even get to Mr. Edwards' store. I told him once that Papa was a WFM member. I wonder if he will still want me to work there.

I t came as no surprise that the company picnic has been cancelled. In church this morning, our pastor talked again about accepting God's will and turning the other cheek. He said that those on strike should remember Jesus' suffering and be peaceful in all they do.

Big Annie led another parade carrying that huge flag. She had two girls about my age holding streamers that came from the top of the flagpole. Papa said the whole family should march today. We were all in our church clothes, and it was peaceful.

Many people cheered and clapped as we walked by in silence. One of the banners said, "Good Enough to Work for Mine Operators, but Not Good Enough to Talk to Them."

There were others who cursed at us and shouted terrible insults. I saw James Richards in the crowd. He shouted, "Why don't you all go back to Finland!"

I felt like shouting back that I am an American, but I remembered what our pastor said. The National Guard soldiers stood everywhere. If those shouting at us came too close, the soldiers stood between and told them to stand back. Some soldiers saluted as our men walked by. Other soldiers looked at the striking men with steel-cold eyes, like they were daring our men to make a wrong move so they could shoot.

"Don't look at anyone," Papa whispered. "Look straight ahead."

After the parade, Papa went to a union meeting. He told us that Sheriff Cruse and the mine managers have hired even more deputies. Some of them work for a company called Waddell-Mahon. Papa said union officials call these men Waddies and that they worked to break the strikes in the western mines. MacNaughton said in the newspaper that he had not authorized Sheriff Cruse to hire these men and that he would pay to send them back. Sheriff Cruse said the violence soured local men on working as deputies, and he had no choice.

"If you ask me," Papa said, "Both Cruse and Mac-Naughton say one thing to each other and another to the newspapers."

Papa said they had talked about the men who will not honor the strike. "I don't like how this strike began, but I will not turn my back on it now." After saying that, Papa and Jaako got up from the table and went outside to finish building the rabbit hutch. On the way out, Papa said, "Most of our men think those who don't honor the strike are the worst kind of traitors."

Monday, July 28

Jenni, Katri and I went blueberry picking. They ate almost as many as they put in their buckets. "Don't eat so many," I said. "We need them for winter."

Our buckets were not yet full at noon, so I took out the bread and *juustoa* Mama had given me, and the canteen of water. Jenni and Katri picked more after that. We got home in the middle of the afternoon. Mama crushed some ice and gave us each a handful of berries to eat with the ice. It tasted so good after being in the hot sun all day.

I asked Mama if I had time to go over to Laurium before supper. She seemed to know what I needed to do and nodded her head. My stomach felt all knotted up as I got closer to Mr. Edwards' store. I tried to think what I should say.

Luckily, only Mr. Edwards was in the shop when I went in the front door. He was standing behind the meat counter. I walked up to him, looked at the floor and said, "Mr. Edwards, I am very sorry I did not come last Friday. I understand if you don't want me to work for you any more."

He came out from behind the meat counter and put his hands gently on my shoulders. "Emma, I am very glad to see you. I was worried you might have been hurt. Of course, I still want you to come every Friday."

I looked up and smiled.

"You haven't told me much about your family," Mr. Edwards said. "Since it's a quiet afternoon, will you tell me now?"

I sat behind the counter on the other stool and told him about Mama, Papa, and everybody. He smiled when I said that Matti was out in the Trap Rock Valley helping Mr. Lamppa on his farm and how all of us were working at whatever we could. I told him about Papa's dream to buy his own farm.

He asked if I had time to sweep out the storeroom before I had to go. I was glad to do it. When I finished, he handed me a loaf of bread and said, "It's a little dry, but it will make good toast."

"That's all right, Sir," I said. "We like it dry to dunk in coffee or hot milk. See you next Friday."

Happier thoughts than I have had all week ran through my mind as I walked home until I came near where Red Jacket Road comes into Calumet Ave. Soldiers and deputies were everywhere! They shouted for people to get back. Some people did and some didn't. I stopped right where I was, too scared to go on, and too scared to run away. I smashed the loaf of bread hugging it, in spite of how dry and hard it was.

A hand touched my shoulder and I nearly jumped out of my skin!

"Emma, what are you doing here?"

I turned and, thank God, it was Mrs. Aittamaa. I told her where I had been and asked what was going on.

The Miscowaubik Club was a social club for mine owners and managers, businessmen, and other professionals. The word "miscowaubik" is Native American for "copper." *Photo RR*

"The men guard the Miscowaubic Club because there was a rumor that someone wanted to blow it up. So far, nothing has happened. Come, I'll show you a short cut across the fields and another street we can take to get home."

On the way, I asked what the Miscowaubic Club was. Mrs. Aittamaa told me it is a building that looks like a fancy house. All the company managers go there to talk or smoke and play cards and other games. Other times they take their wives there to fancy parties. "You have to be rich to get in," she said.

Thursday, July 31

It is hot and the black flies bite horribly. Blueberries grow so close to the ground. We have to bend way over or kneel down to pick them. They are so little— about the size of my baby fingernail. It takes a million of them to fill up a bucket. Katri and Jenni whine all the time and still eat as many blueberries as they put in their buckets. But it is safe and peaceful. For the first time, I like picking blueberries. Everybody seems to be watching all the goings-on with the strike, so there are few others picking. That is fine with me—all the more for us.

Mama thought of another way she could make some money. She reminded Papa about how she used to weave rag rugs back in Finland. If Papa can find the right size pieces of wood, he will try to build her a small loom to do that here.

Each night at supper, there is more bad news. Tonight, Papa told us about something that happened out at Wolverine. Deputies tried to arrest some man at a boarding house because he attacked somebody. The man's wife threw hot water and red pepper at the deputy. Then a whole lot of people rushed at the deputy and his posse and attacked them. It took two squads of militiamen to rescue the law officers. The lady at the boarding house said deputies knocked her down and dragged her by her hair when she told them to leave. She said the soldiers hit her legs and feet with their bayonets. Shots rang out. Papa said he heard the man had been hiding in the closet and had no gun.

Well, if he didn't, then the deputies must have fired theirs. Anyway, they finally arrested the man. The last Papa had heard, the man had been beaten in jail by deputies using things Papa called brass knuckles.

Jenni asked what those were, but Mama said, "No more talk about this now!" She got us all busy washing the dishes. At least Papa stays away from the fighting. But he marches every morning with the men. Big Annie always leads. When the marching ends, Papa stays around the union hall or the Palestra in Laurium and just listens to what is going on.

I tried to sort it all out in my mind by reading the newspaper when I went to the outhouse. The paper said men are fighting each other everywhere. There was a rumor that strikers would try to blow up the bridge between Houghton and Hancock. Strikers threw rocks and swung shovels and rakes at soldiers and lawmen. Deputies and soldiers held their bayonets ready and some fired shots into the air right above the heads of the strikers.

———◆———

National Guard camped, probably in Agassiz Park. St. Joseph's/St. Paul's twin spires show in the background. *Photo J. W. Nara original.*

Mr. Mahoney of the WFM tried to get Governor Ferris to come up here and help settle things. The paper said Governor Ferris will not come, but he wants to treat both sides fairly. He called for a meeting between the companies and the WFM. Union people were glad to hear that and said they would come. The company managers refused! They say they will not meet with any union at all. Every mine location has had fighting. Strikers try to beat up those who will not strike and then the soldiers beat up the strikers.

I hate all of them! I sat in the outhouse and cried until my nose was all stuffed up. I blew my nose into the newspaper, wiped my bottom with it and threw it into the stink.

The railroad into Calumet goes by the bottom of Swedetown hill. There is a bridge over it, which is why the street one block over from ours is called Bridge Street. Jaako and I stood there a little while before he left to spend the day fishing. This morning the train was loaded with men leaving the area. Some even hung out the doors it was so crowded.

"Where are they going?" I asked Jaako.

"Lots of the men who won't strike with us are leaving to find work someplace else."

"Well, I suppose if they have families to feed."

Jaako spat down at the roof of the train. "We are feeding our family aren't we? We are sticking together and helping other families, too. Those men—they got no *sisu*."

Jaako rubbed my head and left to fish. I went back to our house. Mama wanted to take me with her to the Women's Auxiliary meeting. She said Jenni and Katri could take care of themselves for a little while.

Some of the women hugged each other when we arrived. Everyone smiled, and Mama introduced me. Others passed out tea to drink and little cakes to go with it. Mama has been working on her English since she joined.

She understands a lot more, so I did not have to translate as much when Big Annie talked to everybody.

A lady named Mother Jones is coming to help with the strike. Mother Jones has worked a lot with the United Mine Workers. She has been all over the country helping striking men in the Pennsylvania and West Virginia coal mines. The ladies want to be sure there will be a big welcome for her at the train station when she arrives. Big Annie said again how important the women are. She looked around at everyone at the meeting and pointed to me and some other girls with their mothers. A lot of ladies said that if women want their daughters to have a better life than they have, we must stick together. In the end, everything they do is for their children.

There was a social after the meeting. Big Annie walked up to me and asked, "Emma, would you would like to hold one of the streamers on the flag in this Sunday's march?"

Imagine that! She wanted **me** to walk with her at the head of the parade. I think my smile almost burst my face. "It would be an honor," I said.

"Do you have a white dress?"

"Yes, yes, I do," I said. "I will wear my confirmation dress."

Later, Mr. Edwards was glad to see me. He was very busy helping people and so was I. It seems he is getting a lot of business from the WFM. Somebody saw his sign for Finnish speaking people and spread the word around. I whistled and hummed all afternoon as I swept the storeroom floor and sorted through two bushels of onions. I did not even care that the onions stank to high heaven. I lugged home some wilted lettuce for the rabbits and ten pounds of flour for us.

— ⬦ —

Sunday, August 3

I could hardly keep my mind on our pastor's words to
day. He said something about remaining calm.
Yesterday's paper was full of reports of violence by both
the strikers and militia, who have help from the Waddies,
of course. Papa and Jaako talked of nothing else at supper
last night, especially the part where Mr. MacNaughton
said grass would grow in the streets of Calumet before he
would recognize any union. Today I did not think about
that. I was as squirmy as Katri thinking about the parade.

We did not stop to talk with our friends after the
service, but went right to the place where the march would
start. Papa said he was proud of me. He will be with the
rest of the family farther back. Big Annie must be a strong
woman. That huge flag looked very heavy, yet she picked it
up easily, braced it against her stomach and nodded to me
and the other girl she chose for this week. I did not know
her before, and she is older than I am. As we started out, I
felt like I do on the first sunny day after a long winter.

The first few blocks went very well. Then I saw James
Richards standing in the crowd, jeering at everyone in the
parade. He had a rotten tomato in his hand. At that moment, he saw me. He yelled horrible words I would never

repeat to anyone. The tomato flew from his hand and hit me right across my chest!

I wanted to stop right there and scream. Somehow, I managed to keep moving. The red juices ran down my dress. I bit my lip and held my head high.

"Now you're a Red Finn!" he yelled at me.

Big Annie looked toward me. She did not say anything, but I could see in her eyes that she was sad. She nodded in a way that seemed to say, "Don't lower yourself by saying anything back."

I saw Marie farther back in the crowd. She was crying and tapped her hand to her heart. I let a few tears roll down my cheeks, but still kept my head high.

After the parade, Mama said I should not worry about it. She put my dress in cold water with some bleach. "This and the sun should get it out. If it doesn't, I will get some dye and you will have a beautiful green dress."

When I had changed clothes and came downstairs, Papa put his hands on my shoulders and said, "You found your *sisu* today, Emma."

Women marching in a parade. In the scene described, "Big Annie" would have been in the center and Emma on one of the sides holding the streamer attached to the top of the flag pole.
Photo MTU

Monday, August 4

———◦◦◦———

S o many things are happening at once now. It is hard to know what to believe. Mr. Mahoney, who is vice president of the WFM, told the men that many of the newspapers are a "kept press." It's like my papa said; they only say what the company wants them to say. I am finding that the things Papa says, what I hear as people shop in Mr. Edwards' store, or wherever else I go are never the same. I am going to try to put it down my own way to sort it out.

A lot of men who want to go back to work crammed into the Red Jacket Town Hall for a meeting. I guess they think the WFM is not doing a good enough job. They chose eighteen men who speak different languages besides English: Finns, Norwegians, Swedes, Germans, Poles, Croatians, Italians and some more. That was so they can all go back to their own groups and tell them what is going on. They said maybe if people not from the union talked to the C&H managers, they might listen.

That committee asked for even more from C&H than the union was asking. They wanted $3.00 a day for trammers like my father, $3.50 a day for miners and an eight-hour work day. Then they asked for the men to get paid for six shifts every week, but only work five.

Of course, Mr. MacNaughton refused. He probably thinks if he gives the men anything at all, the WFM will take the credit. They all went back to the Washington School for another meeting and formed another committee.

Papa says those other committees only make things worse. He says it shows the company that the men are not united. The company will think they just have to wait long enough for us to give up. I am afraid he might be right. Also, I think the different newspapers each write part of the truth, the part they think is most important. So I will keep reading several papers and think for myself.

We hear shots so often after dark now that I do not even jump anymore. I am still very afraid, but I cannot do anything about it. Jenni told me she pretends they are firecrackers left from the Fourth of July. I put my arms around Katri and told her not to worry.

<hr />

Tuesday, August 5

Today was a day to make me feel better because Mother Jones arrived. A huge crowd greeted her at the station. Not only the striking men and their families, but many other people from all around came. Mother Jones is eighty years old, but you would never know it. She got off the train and walked with no help from the station to the WFM offices.

Mother Jones and Guy Miller at the head of a parade.
Photo MTU

When she got there, she sat down in a rocking chair they had for her and talked to all of us. The newspaper men asked her a lot of questions. I wished I had paper and a pencil like they did.

She told us that there is a lot of fun in life and we do not have to take the sour. Strikes are great fun for her. She said she is proud to be a socialist because they help the working men. She said if working men used their votes the right way, we would not have a governor who sent soldiers to break a strike. She feels the soldiers have no business here because this is an industrial problem, not a revolution. She admitted she was tired and told everyone she would give a speech tomorrow. I wish I could remember more of what she said. I think I will wait until after her speeches to write more. I will go to the library and read several different papers again.

Jenni and Katri have both outgrown their shoes. We go barefoot a lot of the time, but we must wear shoes for church. Mama cut open the ends of their shoes so their toes stuck out. Katri started to giggle, and we all laughed.

"This will not do," Mama said. She dug through her rag bag to find scraps about the same color as their shoes. She mixed up a little flour and water paste and glued the cloth carefully over the top of the end and into the bottom of the shoe to cover their toes.

She looked at me. "Let's have a look at yours, Emma."

I didn't think mine were very bad so I said, "Mine still fit."

"Let me look anyway."

I did not want to, but I sat down in a kitchen chair and held up my feet.

"How long have you been walking around with these big holes in the soles?" she asked me. I shrugged my shoulders.

Mama put her hands on her hips and sighed. We were all quiet for a minute. Then she smiled at me and said. "See if you can find some cardboard."

I went to the cow shed and came back with an empty feed sack. "We do not have any boxes," I said.

Mama looked at the sack. She traced around my shoes, cut two soles for each foot, pasted them together and pasted them inside my shoes. "There, that should help when you walk to Mr. Edwards' store. Try to bring home any old boxes he might throw away. I think Papa has holes in his shoes, too. When I finish the first rag rug, I'll try to sell it for enough to buy some shoes at the second-hand store."

Thursday, August 7

M y feelings have been so mixed up lately. It is something like this. When I was little, I used to run down the grassy side of our hill for the joy of feeling the wind in my face, almost like I was flying. I saw only the green grass and smelled the sweet clover as I tumbled down at the bottom. Nowadays, I drag my way back up Bridge Street and all I see are dingy gray houses. I wish I could be a little girl again. But Mother Jones' speeches and the parades the last two days have helped me see that things can be both gray and green.

The parade yesterday started at the WFM office and went over to the Palestra. The women had made some more banners for the men to carry.

"Ferris will hear from 18,000 miners on election day."

"We demand an eight-hour day and a minimum wage schedule."

"Richest mines but poorest miners."

"The one-man drill, our agitator."

The soldiers were there, and the deputies, too, but there was no trouble.

I took my journal to the library to read the papers. Like the newspaper reporters, I copied the parts of Mother

Jones' speech out of all the papers that I think are the most important.

View from the top of the water tower in Swedetown. "Company Housing" (homes like Emma's) occupies the lower half of the photo. A mine shaft and related buildings are in the center. The single spire of St. Anne's Church appears on the horizon behind the mine hoist building. *Photo MTU*

"I want you to use your brains, not your hands. Your masters want you to use your hands. I see they have the militia up here to take good care of you. The militia loves you dearly. You make the guns and the bayonets, and they've got to be used on you. I've had experience with the militia. They're not bad fellows. . . . Washington and Lincoln didn't want the militia. We didn't have the militia in their days. . . . We were Americans then. What's the matter with you fellows? Why don't you elect the right men to public office? . . . You elected a scab governor to bring out the militia and camp on company ground and take care of company property. This ground belongs to you. . . . Don't carry a gun or a pistol. Let the other fellow do that. Use your two fists and black out his eyes. Then he can't see to shoot you. . . . You don't need to have a fight here. Just be firm and peaceful. They can't operate the mines without you. . . . Just use your brains and wake up to the fact that you have the power . . . The stars and stripes shall float in Calumet and all of Michigan over free workingmen."

Even though she only used the word "men" when she spoke, I think she means all of it to be for women and even girls like me, too. Later, she told the men that whenever she helps out in a strike, she finds that judges and governors guard the wishes of the people with money. I didn't like what she said about fighting, so I'm glad she also told us to be firm and peaceful. She told the men to stand firm and hold out to get what they want.

I went out and sat beside Papa on the front steps after supper. "What do you think about Mother Jones?" I asked him.

"Most of what she says is good," he told me, "But I will never vote for the socialists."

If Papa can see some good and some bad, then I guess I can, too. The green is like the good and the gray is like the bad. The world is full of both.

Monday, August 11

A little good news today. Things have settled down enough that Governor Ferris recalled a lot of the troops. Only a bit over half will be left after today. The WFM has started its own newspaper called the *Miner's Bulletin*. But I still must read the other papers and try to see which I believe more.

Why does bad news always come right after good? Yesterday, one of the remaining soldiers was attacked. He is still alive, but it has turned people against the strike even more. Over 1000 men have given up and gone back to work. Many more have signed petitions to go back under protection. That is enough for C&H to open the mines and bring up rock again. There are rumors that those staying out on strike may not be allowed back to work. What will happen to my family then?

Friday, August 15

I thought this strike could not get any worse but it has. They murdered two men in Seeberville last evening! Just shot them down for no more than walking down a path everybody used there. Not just WFM members, but lots of people are horrified.

The site of the Seeberville shootings in August 1913. This photo, however, was taken during the winter. *Photo MTU*

Everyone who came into Mr. Edwards' store today had something to say about it. Finnish-speaking women told me about how the two men were just taking a short cut—

the same path they have always taken home. Company deputies yelled and told them not to take the path, but they did anyway. The company sent six men, four of them Waddies, to the boarding house where the men lived to bring them to the owners for trespassing. These men who guard are not police officers. How can they tell someone to go with them like they are being arrested? When the men refused to go with them, a fight broke out.

The deputies started shooting into open windows, through the door, not even looking where they shot, or caring that there were people in the house. Nobody in that house had a gun or anything. The lady of the house had a little baby. As she tried to escape, a bullet just missed the baby. It left a burn from the gunpowder on the baby's face!

Several of the Finnish-speaking women said that they heard Sheriff Cruse let the men who did the shooting escape.

The mine managers' wives, and other high class people who live in Laurium, had a different story to tell. They said someone in the house started shooting first. Several said the deputies had a right to defend themselves.

In all, four men got shot. Three died right away. Another died today in the hospital. One thing is certain: Sheriff Cruse has not arrested anyone yet.

One lady came into the store all dressed up in the latest fashions. Her voice was shrill as she told what she had heard. Mr. Edwards sent me into the back room to sweep, but I could still hear her. "It's a shame some innocent people were hurt, but those strikers got what they deserved!"

It is a good thing I was not out there. I thought I would throw up. All Mr. Edwards said to her was, "Who knows what to think these days?"

All afternoon he said similar things, not really agreeing or disagreeing with anyone. I was a bit afraid to speak my mind, but I did anyway since he had asked me to stay until closing.

"Mr. Edwards, what do you really think about the murders?" I asked. "Some of those people said terrible things."

"Sit down for a minute, Emma," he said. "Right now, I'm not sure what to think. I have learned that what causes the most trouble is when people jump into things before they know all the facts. People **react**, instead of thinking. What happened in Seeberville is a sad example of that. I try to wait until things becomes more clear before I do, or say, anything."

I nodded. "May I ask you something else?"

"Of course."

"How can you be so calm with everybody who comes in? So many people came in angry, but they were all right when they left."

Mr. Edwards took his pipe out of his pocket, filled and lit it before he said, "If I want to keep all my customers, they must want to come back, so I try not to take sides. Most folks don't really want to hear what I have to say. They just want to talk, so I listen. Once they have gotten it out, they are fine."

He patted my back then, and I smiled. He also said that from now on, he wants me to arrive at noon and stay until closing. I carried another ten pounds of flour, a loaf of dried bread, and some penny candy home for my sisters. It was a heavy load, and I stopped to rest several times. By the time I got to the library it was past closing time, so I did not get to see Marie.

I wish the mine managers were like Mr. Edwards.

Sunday, August 24

S o much has happened lately that Jenni, Katri and I nearly missed the thimbleberry season. Thimble berry bushes have really big leaves, like giant maple leaves, soft as velvet and darker green, but the berries are the worst to pick. The bushes always seem to grow in hard to reach places, like the sides of steep hills and stream banks. The bushes also have thorny sorts of stems that tear at your clothes. The berries are something like a raspberry and very sweet. When you pick one, it will fit over the end of your finger like a thimble. Anyway, we went picking a few days right at the end of the season.

We came home bruised from slipping and falling down a few stream banks, and scratched from the rough stems, but we got a pail full. In a way, picking thimbleberries was better than listening to more news about people fighting at the mines.

Mama and Papa do not say much, but they are really worried about money. In this first month, no money promised by the WFM has come. Today, Papa came home from the parade and meeting with some news. The union has assessed all its other members around the country $2 per month to help with the strike here. A man and wife here are supposed to get $4 per week. Those with children would get 50 cents more for each child. That would mean our family would get $5.50 a week. Jaako would get $3 each week as a single man. None of the money has come yet. Mama pressed her lips together and turned back to stirring the pot of soup on the stove.

With so little to expect in strike benefits, I wish we had picked more thimbleberries.

M ama left my sisters and me at home today and went to march with Papa. She said we were to pick tomatoes and green beans in the garden and get everything ready for canning. We carried up all the empty jars and top bands from the cellar and washed them. Mama told me to use boiling water to rinse them. Jenni and Katri washed and snapped green beans. I scalded and peeled a bushel of tomatoes and packed them into the jars.

By the time Mama got home, we had lots of jars waiting for her. She put two big kettles full of water on the stove, screwed the bands and lids down tight on the tomatoes and put them into the kettles of water. The boiling water around the jars will cook the tomatoes and seal the lids. She did the green beans a little differently. First, she sprinkled a bit of salt over the beans, added a piece of bacon to the top, and poured in boiling water to fill the jar. She screwed the lids and bands on tight, so they were ready for the boiling kettles.

All afternoon, the kettles boiled. The minute Mama pulled out one batch of jars with tongs, she put more in, adding water to the kettle whenever it did not come up to the neck of the jars. I hauled in bucket after bucket of water from the pump. Mama kept Jenni and Katri busy hauling in more wood and coal for the stove.

Between the sun beating down on the house and the street, and the heat from the stove, all our dresses were wringing wet with sweat. Last year on canning days, Mama made ice cream when we finished. Today, she let us shave some ice from the block in the icebox, but we only got a teaspoon of maple syrup to put on it.

Jaako came home with only one small fish today. He said there are too many people trying to do the same thing. Mama cut up the fish for tonight's *mojakka* and added more water and another potato.

Papa has started trying to speak English more so he can get better at it. "Dat man name of Judge Murphy what Governor Ferris sent up here—'sposed to see what goes on told what he found out. Guess he really got on da company men when they don't see him las week, him being da governor's man and all. Anyway, he not to talk about da WFM."

Then Papa got tired of trying to think of the words he needed, so he went back to Finnish. He said Murphy sent his report to Governor Ferris. The report said that our men have real grievances and the company managers do treat some men unfairly. It said our men were entitled to some of what they are asking for. Murphy also said he thinks the state will have to leave National Guard troops here for some time.

Mama asked if Papa wanted another bowl of stew. He usually eats two or three bowls. Papa said he was quite full, but I think he wanted to leave more for the rest of us. He got up and went to sit on the front steps.

I went out and sat beside him when we finished the dishes. "Papa, tell me true," I said, "is the strike going to last a lot longer?"

He patted my back and said, "I'm afraid so, but don't you worry about it."

Even though Papa told me that, I am worried. I know what I must do to help, and I am not going to ask Mama or Papa first.

I left a bit earlier than usual for Mr. Edwards' store today so I could stop at the main school office on my way. I needed to be sure they will have evening classes again this year for people who are working but want to finish grades seven and eight.

I waited until it was quiet in the middle of the afternoon to ask Mr. Edwards. My heart pounded. I stood with my hands behind me so he would not see my hands shaking. "Mr. Edwards," I said. "Do you know of any family who might need help? You know I am a good worker. I can help cook, clean, do washing and ironing. I can mind children. I can sew a little. I would like to work more days each week for pay."

"Are things that hard at home?"

I nodded and told him what we are doing, but that it is not enough. "I hate to see Mama spend the money for the farm. I am strong, and I can work to help."

"Shouldn't you be going back to school in a few weeks?"

"I can go to evening classes."

"Well, you are pretty young to work as a maid, but let me think about who I know."

I went about my usual tasks feeling hopeful.

About an hour before closing, Mr. Edwards handed me a sealed envelope. It had an address on Kearsarge Street on it. "Take this letter and give it to the lady of the house."

This home on Iroquois St. in Laurium is typical of the "upper class" of mine managers and owners, successful businessmen, and professionals. *Photo MTU-N*

There are many grand houses in Laurium. That is where most of the mine captains, managers and business people live. The house I went to was not the grandest house on the street, but I think three company houses like ours would easily fit inside it. I stood in front of it a moment just looking at the roofed front porch and all the fine carving around the windows and roof. There were even lace curtains on the attic windows.

I gulped and walked up to the front door. *I have sisu,* I said over and over to myself. A woman wearing a maid's cap and apron answered the door. "Excuse me," I said, "Mr. Edwards asked me to take this letter to the lady of the house."

"Come with me then."

I followed her through the entry way and into a large parlor facing the street. Oh, the furnishings were grand, and there was a large carpet in the middle of the floor. So much beautiful woodwork, all of it shiny. The lady of the house sat in one of the chairs sipping tea from the daintiest cup I ever saw. I did my best curtsey and held out the letter. She smiled and took it.

When she finished reading it, she smiled at me again and said, "Well, Emma, Mr. Edwards likes his coffee promptly at seven o'clock standard time, so you will need to be here by 6:30."

I almost fell over! Mr. Edwards had sent me to his own house.

"Yes, of course, I can be here then. Thank you very much, ma'am."

"Since you are just starting out and will need quite a bit of training, we will pay twenty-five cents a day. Half of the first week will cover the cost of your caps and aprons. You'll help Maude Monday through Friday. Mr. Edwards says he wants you in the grocery all day Saturday. I shall see you in the morning."

I wanted to jump up and yell, "Hurray!" but that would have been most unmannerly.

Mrs. Edwards turned to the woman who answered the door. "Maude, please show Emma to the kitchen, so she'll know where to come in tomorrow."

I think I floated all the way home. I burst in the door shouting, "Mama, I have a real job for real pay!"

Mama was certainly surprised. When I promised to go to evening school, she wiped a tear from her eye and gave me a hug. The money I will earn will be exactly enough to pay the rent each month.

Sunday, August 31

W hat a change this job will bring to my life. Mama shook me awake at 5:30 Saturday morning. I dressed quickly and ate some *korppua* and *juustoa* as I walked. It was getting light, but the sun was not yet up. By the time I reached the kitchen door at Mr. Edwards' house, the sun was peeking over the horizon. I was breathless from walking so fast, but I was exactly on time.

Maude handed me a cap and apron and set me right away to grinding the coffee. Mrs. Edwards has her coffee grinder nailed to the kitchen wall. (Ours stays in a cupboard and then sits on the table when we need it.) There is such a pleasant smell to freshly ground coffee.

"Pay attention," Maude said, "to how Mr. Edwards likes his coffee. You'll do this yourself on Monday."

Maude put some ground coffee in the bottom of the pot. Then, and this was the strange part, she broke an egg, added a bit of water and scrambled it. She poured a little of this egg mixture over the coffee grounds and swished the pot around. (She put the rest of the egg mixture in the ice box saying it was for tomorrow and the next day.) She filled the pot with water (how nice to have running water right there in the kitchen—no going out to a pump here) and put it on the stove.

"Watch it carefully, just until it boils. Then take it off, stir it and let it sit for a bit."

The grounds came to the top all together with a little crust. The boiling started at the edges of the pot. I did just as Maude told me. While I watched the coffee, Maude fixed bacon, eggs and muffins. She had me set out dishes on a tray. Oh, such delicate china. I was almost afraid it would break if I touched it. The linen napkin was so fine.

My curiosity made me ask, "Miss Maude, why did you put egg in the coffee?"

"Makes the grounds stay together and settle to the bottom of the pot afterward, so the coffee pours out clearer. You don't have grounds in the bottom of every cup."

At home, we just let the coffee boil for a while. We put up with grounds at the bottom of each cup unless Mama strains it.

When Maude had the breakfast tray ready, she handed it to me and said, "Mr. Edwards takes breakfast in his study—up the stairs, first door on your right." She turned to prepare another tray for Mrs. Edwards.

There are two staircases in Mr. Edwards' house, fancy ones near the front door, and plain ones near the kitchen. I went up the plain ones as I was told. The door to Mr. Edwards' study was opened a bit. That was a good thing because I had both hands on the tray. I hesitated to go in.

"I have your breakfast, Mr. Edwards," I said.

"Come on in," he told me.

I pushed the door with my toe. Mr. Edwards sat at

a large desk. He pushed some papers aside, and I set the tray in front of him.

He smiled at me. "Thank you, Emma."

I smiled back, "You're welcome. And thank *you*."

He nodded, and I went back down to the kitchen.

The rest of the day I was so very busy. Now I know why all the woodwork was so shiny—we polished every bit of it with something called lemon oil. There were so many places that needed a touch with the feather duster. At our house, we fold our cotton napkins up and use them several times until they are really dirty. Here, they use a fresh linen napkin every time, and I ironed a week's worth. Sprinkle the napkin with water, grab a hot iron off the stove, press the napkin, watch out not to scorch the linen, put the cool iron back on the stove to heat and grab the other hot one . . . I thought I would never get through that pile. Dinner was served in the dining room, and later, I took Mrs. Edwards' tea to the parlor.

All day long, Miss Maude kept saying, "Pay attention now . . ." and I did my best.

After we finished the supper dishes (supper was also served in the dining room) we both were sent to Mr. Edwards' study. "Maude, it's quite a long walk back and forth for Emma. I think it might be best if Emma stays with us like you do. I'll get the roll-away bed from the storage closet and set it up. You can show her how to make it up on Monday. If you like, you may hang a curtain between you for privacy."

"Yes, Sir," Maude said as he handed her an envelope with her pay for the week.

"You'll get your first pay next Saturday," he told me. "Bring enough clothing with you for the week when you come on Monday."

Maude was pleasant enough. She offered me plenty to eat when we took our meals in the kitchen, but she glared at me when we walked out the kitchen door. I am not sure she likes me.

I was tired but happy when I got home. Although they had finished their supper too, Mama and Papa had waited for me to come home before going to *sauna*. I told Mama about putting egg in the coffee and the rest of my day while she swatted my back with the *vihta*.

When I told Mama that I would be staying with Mr. and Mrs. Edwards during the week, she wished I didn't have to. Then she turned her back to pour some water onto the hot rocks. Mama said she was happy for me as she turned back, but she wiped her eyes. She said it was sweat.

———◆———

Sunday, September 7

I forgot to put my journal in the bag with my clothes on Monday. Since I did not come home again until Saturday, I had no chance to write. Now there is so much to say, I hardly know where to start.

I cannot believe how kind Mr. and Mrs. Edwards are. I have never eaten so much good food in my life. I have a bed of my very own with a down comforter and a big fluffy pillow. It is right next to the attic window with the lace curtains. Maude did hang a thick cotton drape between her part of the attic bedroom and mine. It is almost like having a room all my own. It did seem strange though not to have Katri and Jenni to curl up with me.

They have electric lights and a toilet inside the house. There is a tank above the toilet full of water. When you pull the chain, the water comes down and flushes out the toilet. It makes such a funny sound.

No wonder rich people need help. There is so much more housework to do. Silver forks, knives, spoons, serving trays and bowls must be polished. Those beautiful carpets are heavy and must be hauled outside, put over the clotheslines and hit all over with a broom to knock the dust out of them. The wood floors must be mopped. All the wood trimming around everything must be dusted and rubbed with lemon oil. Mr. and Mrs. Edwards wear fresh clothes each morning so there is a lot of laundry to wash, hang out, and iron. Maude cooks and bakes like every day is Sunday.

I found out why Maude didn't seem to like me. I overheard her ask Mrs. Edwards if she planned to let her go after I was trained. Mrs. Edwards told her, "Of course not." So Maude has been friendly towards me ever since. I saw Mr. Edwards only at breakfast and in the evening during the week. Mr. and Mrs. Edwards seem a little younger than my parents, but they have no children, which is sad. I hear them call each other Chester and Jessie, but I would never be so disrespectful as to use their first names.

Almost every day, someone came to tea. Thursday, Mrs. Edwards went out for tea. That was the only time we rested. Maude put her feet up on a kitchen chair. We had currant cookies and lemonade.

On Wednesday, I found two housedresses on my bed when I came up after supper. Maude said she had told Mrs. Edwards how little I had in my bag when I came Monday morning. Mrs. Edwards sent her to the second hand shop with a few coins. "I hope they fit all right," Maude said.

Mr. Edwards let me read his newspaper every evening after he finished it, but it only told the company side of what is going on with the strike. I had to wait until Saturday when I worked at the grocery store to hear our side. It will be dark soon, so I will sum it up quickly.

Mr. Moyer, the president of the WFM, finally came to the Copper Country. He made a speech on Labor Day. The WFM also has an important lawyer named Clarence Darrow to help our cause. There was a big fight between almost 200 strikers and a lot of deputies at the North Kearsarge mine. A girl just two years older than I am got shot in the head! She is at the Calumet Public Hospital. They do not know if she will live. There was even more fighting after that. Some of the women went so far as to dip their brooms in buckets of filth from an outhouse. They shook the brooms at the scabs (that is what the men who continue to work are called). Two women were taken to jail when they hit some scabs over the head with their brooms.

One Finnish lady told me, "I got little children to feed. My neighbor takes care of them and hers so I can work. We can't let our men give in, now or ever! All this we do, even brooms full of crap, we do for our children. You, too. You deserve a better life."

C&H blames the union and the union blames C&H. People keep saying "shocking lawlessness". I almost feel numb. I followed Mr. Edwards' advice and kept saying, "*Voi tuhanen*, oh my goodness," to everybody.

Yesterday, Governor Ferris finally met with Mr. MacNaughton at Ferris' home in Big Rapids. Many people have said Ferris is on the company side. This time the paper reported that he tried many ways to get MacNaughton to listen, but that stubborn man will not give in even one inch. He will have nothing to do with Mr. Darrow's suggestion to arbitrate. I found out "arbitrate" means each side would choose two representatives. The governor would be a fifth member of the committee who would try to help them work out something between what the union wants and what the company is willing to give.

At closing time on Saturday, Mr. Edwards handed me three quarters. "We agreed that half of your first week's earnings would pay for your caps, aprons and other needed clothes. There is a sack of potatoes by the storeroom door for you, too."

"Thank you very much, sir," I said. I saw some cardboard boxes by the trash bin, so I took them home, too, so Mama can fix our shoes again.

Thursday, September 11

Maude showed me how to carry a tray with one hand, so I can open or close a door with my other hand. I spread my hand wide open and put it flat up against the try a little past the middle. One end of the tray rests on my hand, and the other end of the tray rests on my shoulder. She is also teaching me to sew a fine seam. It surprised me to know that even rich people mend their clothes and darn the holes in their socks. I always thought if you had enough money, you just bought new ones when the old ones wore out. Maude was pleased that I already knew how to put the wooden darning bulb into the heel, run long stitches from one side of the hole to the other and carefully weave new threads back and forth, over and under until the hole is filled.

I don't have to ask Mr. Edwards for the newspaper anymore. He brings it out to the kitchen and hands it to me as soon as he has finished it. This week has been more of the same—marches every day with fights, more women using brooms dipped in outhouse filth, more arrested. I hope my mother has not been with them.

Friday, September 12

I got to see Marie today. In the afternoon, Mrs. Edwards handed me a book. "Mr. Edwards asked if you would return this book to the library and find this other one," she said and handed me his note. "Better run along quickly before the library closes."

I jumped up from the silver polishing and ran right away.

Oh, how Marie and I hugged each other when I found her in the big reading room on the second floor. We whispered our news back and forth. She asked why I have not come lately and told me she has been busy at many of the same tasks at home that I had—picking in the garden, canning, and all that. She also watches her little brother and sisters a lot. I told her about how I am working now.

The last thing she said frightened me. "You are still my best friend, so please, tell your Papá stay away from the front lines of the marches. My papá works in the company carpentry shop. C&H has them making big batting sticks for the deputies to use on the strikers."

Saturday, September 13

Oh, what news came into the store this afternoon! A huge group of strikers, including men who came down here from Keweenaw County, tried to march into Yellow Jacket this morning. Our men have always marched on public streets. Yellow Jacket is on company land, and the soldiers have been guarding it.

One of our men was actually on a horse and started shouting at the soldiers, "You can't stop us." Militiamen rode their horses in front of our men. One man threw down the flag he carried, but another picked it up. A big fight started. A sword ripped through the flag and horses trampled it.

Big Annie picked up another flag and held it across her chest. The lady who told me this was watching from the sidelines and said Big Annie yelled at the soldiers. "Kill me! Run your bayonets and swords through this flag! Kill me! But I won't move back! If this flag will not protect me, then I will die with it."

This lady said Big Annie was still there when she and some of the others backed off. Later, the lady said she was at the Italian Hall and saw the flag with the slash in it. "It was a horrible big cut," she said.

She went on and on about how the soldiers abuse our men as I put her groceries in her mistress' shopping bag. "What could be next?" I said. It was a real question in my mind, and I had to bite my lip not to show my worry.

<hr />

Sunday, September 14

I was so happy to see my family when I got home last evening. I gave Mama a whole dollar and two quarters—my full pay this week. Mama put it in the jar she uses for everyday money. Mr. Edwards had also given me a box with flour, sugar and (a big surprise) a fresh apple for everyone. Oh, how tart, yet sweet they were, crisp and dripping with juice, so much sweeter than the wild crab apples Jenni and Katri have been gathering.

Papa brought more news after he came home from another big meeting at the Palestra. Mr. Moyer has come back to Calumet along with another man, Mr. Lennon of the American Federation of Labor. They told the men to stand firm. Moyer says C&H must recognize the union for the strike to end. Lennon told our men that the copper in the ground here should belong to all the people, not just a few rich men from Boston. I told Papa what Marie had said about the batting sticks.

"We stick to my plan in this family," Papa said. "Anna, I know how you feel, but please, stay away from these marches. I see what the other women do. I don't want you to be hurt. It is enough for me to be there."

The long summer days are over. It was nearly dark

by the time I had to go back to Mr. Edwards' house. Jaako walked with me. When we got to the kitchen door, he put his hands on my shoulders and said, "Don't you worry about us, Emma. You know I will take Papa's place and take care of everybody if I need to."

I thank God for Mr. Edwards and this job. I can read and write here by electric light. I have plenty to eat and my parents have one less belly to fill. My earnings and the food I bring home help my family. We will get through this. We have *sisu*. I must keep telling myself that. But what Jaako said hung in my mind. Does he think something might really happen to Papa?

Thursday, September 18

The papers are still full of what happened last Saturday. The news of Big Annie and the flag went all over the country. Some have even called her a modern Joan of Arc. I am proud to think that I know her and marched at her side that Sunday in August. One report stated that it was a foreign-born militiaman who abused our nation's flag. Mr. Moyer wired Governor Ferris that troops rode down women and children and that it was an officer who tore the flag with his bayonet. I keep trying to remind myself that the truth is probably somewhere between what each side says.

C&H tried to bring in workers from New York this week. The WFM put out signs telling such men not to be scabs. They told these men not to hurt the cause of all workers. Most of the men who arrived in the first trainload listened to the union. They either left our area or joined the union.

My days are full of work, but Mr. Edwards makes sure I finish my duties in time to go to evening classes for seventh grade reading and arithmetic. Most evenings when I finish my studies, I am too tired to do anything but fall into bed.

Friday, September 26

W hat a confusing week this has been. The lawyers hired by all the mining companies are
trying to get the courts onto their side now.
They asked Judge O'Brien to place an injunction on the
strikers saying the men may not picket or march and may
not try to stop men who are not in the union from going to
work. The companies' lawyers say the union is trespassing
and interfering with people's right to work. The judge put
a temporary order on the men but said the companies must
prove their case. Mr. Darrow argued that our men have the
constitutional right to freedom of speech and assembly.

Some of the older students in my evening classes
said that this law firm, Rees, Robinson and Peterman, are
C&H's lawyers and they have a secret agreement with the
mining companies to use the courts to work against the
miners. They are the ones who file complaints and get our
men arrested. I heard they are defending the Wadell men
and deputies accused of the murders in Seeberville.

What I learned about Judge O'Brien is interesting.
He used to work as a lawyer who took C&H and some of
the other companies to court to make them give money to
the families of men who were hurt or killed. He won lots

of cases. C& H has hated Mr. O'Brien for a long time. He seems to be on the side of the strikers. When he was elected a judge, he swore an oath to uphold the law. He is stuck in the middle, a little like King Solomon in the Bible, trying to decide which woman was really that baby's mother. I am glad I am not Judge O'Brien.

A lot of the union men met at the Italian Hall. Papa told me one Finnish man said the Russian Tsar could not have done a better job of taking away the men's rights. Many men continued to march and got arrested. They were set free right away while they wait for a trial at a later time. Papa says he will obey the order not to march. He will wait and hope.

Matti has come home from Mr. Lamppa's farm. Now the cellar is full of potatoes, onions, and turnips. Daisy has all the hay she needs for the winter. Matti tried to find other work in Lake Linden, but that town has a lot of French Canadian people who work at the C&H stamp mill. They are not on strike and don't like those who are. There was no work to be had for the son of a striker, or a Finn for that matter. Papa wanted him to go back to school anyway.

Papa told him, "You go school. Den you want farm wit me, dat good. Or sometin else, dat good too."

For now, I will have to keep serving meals, washing dishes, polishing, mopping floors, beating rugs, reading and studying. I am so tired all I want to do is turn out the light and go to sleep. But I will do my two pages of arithmetic problems and think about seeing my family on Sunday.

Wednesday, October 1

Hurray! Hurray! Judge O'Brien took away the injunction on September 29. He said the men have a constitutional right to march and assemble as long as they are peaceful. Most of the men arrested for marching in spite of the injunction had their cases dismissed. Others received only probation for a sentence. Company lawyers tried to get Judge O'Brien to put out a second injunction, but he rejected it. Company lawyers said they will take the case to the Michigan Supreme Court.

Right away the trouble started again. There was even picketing in Swedetown. Women I know grabbed dinner pails away from scabs and threw their food into the road. Over in Red Jacket, a scab used a club on a woman who took his dinner pail. That started a huge fight, and Big Annie was arrested again. A judge named Fisher charged her with intimidation but let her go after someone paid $300 for her bond. A man in my evening class said she was right back on the picket line at four o'clock this morning. He said he heard Big Annie tell a scab it is blood money scabs work for. She yelled at the men not to go down there and spat at some.

The jail doors bang shut, then open, and shut, and

open again. Men get arrested, judges let them off. C&H cannot rule the courthouse. I hate all this fighting, but at least someone is paying attention to how hard we working people have it.

I have completely missed one of my favorite times of the year—fall. Last year, I walked out into the woods on a Saturday or Sunday afternoon. I remember how crisp the air seemed as the leaves crunched beneath my feet. The sky always has a deeper blue on fall days, a different blue than any other time of the year. The woods are like the warm embers of a fire—red, gold and yellow. Those walks left me feeling full and peaceful. Jenni, Katri and I would make huge piles of leaves and jump into them. The color came this year, but I never got out into the woods. I didn't get to jump into leaves. I only raked up piles in Mr. Edwards' yard and dumped them in the ash can to burn. The smoke stung my eyes and missing the fun stung my heart.

M atti came by Mr. Edwards' kitchen door this evening to tell me he and my sisters skipped school today (even though the truancy officer might come after our family) and marched in their own parade. "Papa is striking for us," was written on the signs he and other children carried.

I told him I was proud of them. I wish I had been there, but I have chosen this path to help my family. Papa always taught us to act on what we believe and finish something we start. I must stick to this job until the strike is over.

A few weeks ago, I saw that awful James Richards again. I thought I would be rid of him at the end of school last June. Then there he was with that rotten tomato he threw at me in the parade. Then there he was, again, walking down the alley. He saw me beating a rug late in the afternoon. He stared at me for a time and then laughed, "Ha, ha, ha! You've found what you're best suited for."

Now he comes by at least every other day to taunt me. I hate that boy but I will not give him the satisfaction of knowing how he hurts my feelings. The rugs got beat really clean, though. I am very fast at taking down the washing if I see him coming.

The Michigan Supreme Court ruled yesterday on the injunction against our men's marching. They said the union men are guaranteed their right to march, speak out and picket, as long as it is peaceful. They may not threaten men who wish to work or harm them in any way. The way things have been I am afraid it will not work. I keep thinking about the things my Papa said about the first day of the strike—so much anger built up into storms and lightning. I am afraid things will stay as they are or get worse. Papa has always been a peaceful man. So are a lot of the others. Why can't they be the leaders? Why won't those "hot heads" listen to men like my papa and act like grown-ups are supposed to?

Sunday, October 12

We had a bit of a celebration at home today. Matti got a deer earlier this week—with a bow and arrow he made during the summer. Just like the Indians used to do. Matti had been practicing all summer shooting at a target whenever he was not doing farm chores. By today, the meat was properly cured, and we had venison roast for dinner with potatoes and turnips and rich brown gravy. There was applesauce for dessert. How good everything tasted. Everyone said it was the best meal they ever had. Mama smiled for the first time in many Sundays. She will put a little more of the meat in the icebox for this week. Jaako and Matti will be busy for the next few days smoking and drying the rest. Papa told them to be sure to take some over to Mr. and Mrs. Aittamaa since they have been so kind in giving us eggs from their chickens.

Sunday, October 19

C&H announced this week through the newspapers that they will begin an eight-hour day in January. In order not to give any credit to the WFM, they stated that this has been the plan for quite some time. There will be no minimum wage and the one-man drill is here to stay. The articles in the papers all week have talked about how well C&H has tried to take care of the workers. The article reminded people that C&H built the library, hospital and bathhouse. A table listed all the mines showing how many had produced more money in copper than the amount of money spent to build the mines, smelters, railroads, buy machinery, and everything else. I was surprised to read that less than twenty mines from the beginning of mining here until 1910 actually paid back more money than what was invested. I still think all the articles were printed to make the company look good and make our men look ungrateful.

C&H and the Quincy Mining Company in Hancock are trying again to bring in new people to work in the mines. Almost as much rock is coming out of the ground as there was before the strike started.

Yesterday, many of the Finnish women who came in

to buy groceries talked about their fear of the Black List. They believe the companies have a list of every striker or anyone who ever caused them trouble. They say the companies share these lists. If a man leaves one company and tries to work at another, company men check this list and will not hire them. The mining companies say this is not true, but everyone knows someone (sometimes they even say the names) who was refused a job in this way. When the strike does end, will Papa and Jaako even be allowed back to work? What will happen if they aren't, and if Papa cannot buy the farmland? The company owns our house. Will we be out in the street? Will I spend all my life polishing someone else's silver?

⟨⬥•⬥⟩

Sunday, October 26

The young men in my reading class say that the strike is lost. The marches accomplish nothing, but the union will fine men who do not participate. It does not take many fines to lose what little is given in strike benefits. Fewer men march in spite of this. More arrests. More short trials. Big Annie was in court again this week and then right back at the head of the parades. More fights and violence. Several volleys of shots were fired at the train today, supposedly by strikers. Mr. Moyer has left the area, so our men are on their own for now.

The rabbits are doing well—one was in the stew today. Katri cried over it because she has been treating the rabbits like pets.

Mama said, "I told you not to play with them. You can eat the stew or go hungry." Katri choked back her tears and ate the stew. Later I told her it was all right because now the rabbit was part of her forever.

I bring home an old box or two every time I can so Mama can keep putting new pieces of cardboard in all our shoes. Papa wears through a layer of cardboard almost every day. He says nothing, but there is always sadness in his eyes. Matti and Jaako try to tell jokes, and they are good ones, but the laughter is not real.

Papa wanted to practice his English again as he walked me back to Mr. Edwards' house. "We got lots *sisu* Emma. You no worry now. I proud you. Mama and me love you. Don't matter we got no *raha*." (That means money.) I smiled before I went in the kitchen door, but my smile was only on the outside.

——◆——

Today as we walked home from church, a union man Papa does not know all that well came up to him. He asked Papa how he felt about the strike and if he wanted to leave the union and go back to work.

"I heard someone would be coming around," Papa said in Finnish. "So here's what I say. I don't like everything about the WFM, but if some of us quit now, it will be bad for everybody. We have to stick together! If we don't speak with one voice, we get nothing. I will see this thing through to the end for the sake of all the others."

The man shook Papa's hand, thanked him and walked away. Mama raised her eyebrows and looked at Papa. He sighed and kept talking in Finnish, "Anna, that's the truth, and you know it. The company can see how divided we are. They use that against us. This bickering back and forth between the socialist Finns and the rest of us makes all of us weaker."

A burst of wind whistled out of the north and blew a few old dried-out leaves down the street. I shivered.

Saturday, November 8

Winter's first blast hit us today. The wind was so strong the snow seemed to come sideways. I was numb from cold walking the few blocks from the store back to Mr. Edwards' house. By the time Maude and I finished washing the supper dishes, there were drifts in the street.

"Emma, I won't even think of you walking home in this weather," Mr. Edwards said. "I will take you home in our carriage."

Mrs. Edwards bundled me up in an extra blanket. "Thank you, ma'am," I said, pulling it tight around my face.

"Do be careful," she told Mr. Edwards as he tied a scarf over his nose and mouth.

He nodded, and we were off.

It was the first time I have ever ridden in such a fancy carriage, and it was exciting in spite of the blizzard. The lantern danced on its high pole and the wick blew out. Mr. Edwards did not try to relight it since it was not helping much anyway. The street lights lit our way through Laurium and Red Jacket, but the road to Swedetown was black as pitch. We were lucky that another wagon was ahead of us. We stayed right in its track.

"You'll never get the carriage up the hill at Bridge Street," I said. "Drop me off at the bottom. You can turn easily there, and it is only a few blocks up to my house. I can make it home all right. You can follow your own track back to Red Jacket."

"Are you sure?"

"Yes."

"All right then. If the weather doesn't break by tomorrow evening, don't try to come back. Stay at home until the storm ends."

"Thank you," I said and turned into the night. I walked up the hill backwards so the wind would not be in my face.

Mama and Papa were very glad to see me when I came in the door. I told them about my carriage ride while I drank hot milk and warmed myself by the kitchen stove. The fire is nearly out now, and I can barely see. Mama is ready to put hot coals in the bed warmers so we will be warm all night.

<hr/>

Sunday, November 9

S now was still falling fast this morning. We did not even try to go to church. Papa read from the Bible, and we said our prayers at home. There was enough to eat at dinner. The WFM finally came through on its promise to help our men. But instead of cash payments, they gave out coupons to spend at the union commissary. Papa said everybody was upset about that. He and Mama like to shop at the Finnish stores to support our own. He heard the men out at Wolverine were upset because they have a co-op and could not spend their coupons there.

Mama reminded him that this help was better than nothing, especially since her rag rugs are not selling so well. Too many women are trying to do the same thing. She used all Papa's and Jaako's shares to buy flour, lard, candles, and some almost-as-good-as-new shoes for all of us.

The storm finally stopped in the afternoon. The sun shone so bright it almost hurt my eyes. We older children met in the field below our house (where we played stickball all summer) and we had a grand snow ball fight. I got hit by several, but it didn't hurt. I hit lots of the others with my snowballs, too.

When it came time for me to head back to Mr.

Edwards' house, Papa brought me an extra pair of his wool socks.

"Put these on over your shoes," he said. "It will keep your feet warmer. I'm sorry we could not get galoshes to wear in the snow."

The snow stuck to the socks, but my feet were warmer. "The shoes are just as good," I said.

Thursday, November 13

I s everyone truly against us? This week the *Calumet News* printed a membership form for something called the Citizen's Alliance. The membership pledge said they believe that the WFM are all agitators and that they have forced themselves upon our community long enough. The pledge also said the union has attacked people, spread the poison of socialism, violence, and fear, and has not paid attention to the law. It urged good citizens to become active against the strike.

All week the *Calumet News* and the *Daily Mining Gazette* have said everything evil about people like my father. The miner's bulletin, *Truth*, calls the other papers liars. I try so hard to sort out what is true, but I feel lost inside.

If that was not enough, Big Annie was convicted of assault in court Monday. Even though she only served a few days in jail, it is like a slap in the face to all of us. People against the strike have committed assault too, but none of them have been arrested and jailed. It is all so unfair.

It seems like everyone on both sides is yelling so loudly, they cannot even hear themselves. I wish I could put my hands over my ears and scream at everyone, "Be quiet! Be quiet and listen," but they probably would not hear me either.

This evening when Mr. Edwards came home, he slipped something white into his coat pocket. When I hung his coat in the closet for him, I put my hand in to see what it was. It was his Citizen's Alliance button. I said nothing. I suppose he must join to keep his regular customers. The union people he was selling to at a discount must shop at the union commissary now, so business has dropped a bit. But seeing it still hurt.

Sunday, November 16

Last night after I got home, I heard Papa tell Mama that he heard the Mohawk Mining Company had threatened to evict people from their company houses if the rent was not paid. "Do you think C&H will do that?" I heard Mama ask.

"I hope not," Papa said. "I hate to see Emma working. I wish she had stayed in school, but she makes just enough to keep our rent paid. I am thankful for that." Somehow my bed felt warmer, even though Jenni, Katri and I were huddled together and shivering.

After church this morning, Papa decided to write a letter to the paper saying not all union men are socialists. He wrote it in Finnish and asked me to translate it for him. Here is what he said: *I am on strike, but I am not a socialist. I am a hard-working man trying to provide for my family. I am not a violent man. Please believe WFM members are not bad people. Most of them are like me. We just want something better for our families. That is why we came to this country. Joseph Niemi, Swedetown.*

When I finished the translation, I wrote *translated by Emma Niemi* and signed my name. I hope the paper prints it.

Friday, November 21

————◆————

My head still hurts, but the long talk afterward with Mr. Edwards made my heart hurt less.

It was already dark when I left the store at closing time. Mr. Edwards told me he had a bit of book-keeping to do and that I should tell Mrs. Edwards he would be home in a little while. Most of the snow from the blizzard has melted, but the slushy puddles freeze again as soon as the sun goes down.

I was about half way back to Mr. Edwards' house when I noticed someone following me. I quickened my pace. Then the taunting started. "Red Finn, red Finn, send you to the coal bin."

It was that awful James Richards!

He did not stop with words this time. He jumped on me and pushed me into a slushy puddle—rubbed my face right in it. I screamed. He kept pushing. The ice cut my face and the frigid water soaked right through my coat.

Just as suddenly, someone grabbed James! "You good-for-nothing pile of horse manure!" I heard. "If I ever catch you doing this to Miss Niemi, or any other girl, again, I won't bother to tell your father, I'll thrash you myself."

It was Mr. Edwards. He held James by the ear with

one hand and helped me up with the other. "You will apologize this instant," he told James.

James looked at the street and muttered, "Sorry."

"Not good enough," Mr. Edwards said. He pulled on James' ear harder, and James began to cry.

"Repeat after me. 'Miss Niemi.'"

"Miss Niemi," James said in a dry whisper.

"I have forgotten my manners and am acting like an idiot. Please forgive me."

James actually repeated it! My mouth dropped open, and I nodded.

Mr. Edwards gave him a kick in the pants. "Now get out of my sight, you sorry excuse of a young man."

Mr. Edwards helped me walk into the house and called to Mrs. Edwards. She held up her hand to her mouth when she saw me. Mr. Edwards explained while Mrs. Edwards helped me out of my coat and upstairs to the bathroom. She called to Maude to draw me a hot bath while she dressed the cut on my face.

Dinner was very late, and I did not serve it. I warmed my bones in the tub of hot water. Maude brought me a cup of tea, fresh towels and clean clothes. After I dressed and came down to the kitchen, Maude gave me a dinner plate she had kept warm. "I'll be up in our room if you want to talk later," she said.

I thanked her and tried to eat a little. Mr. Edwards came into the kitchen.

"Are you feeling better?" he asked.

I nodded and said, "I don't understand why he hates me so." I told him about some of the things that had happened in school and how James used to come down the alley during the fall and tease me.

"Let me tell you about him. James' grandfather and my father came from Cornwall, England, on the same boat. They both dug tons of rock out of the Central Mine back in the eighties. They were good miners, so when Central shut down, C&H hired them and by 1900, both of them were captains.

"They vowed their sons should have a better life, so they saved every extra penny to send us to college. My father sent me to the University of Michigan to learn about business. James' grandfather sent his father over to Houghton to the Michigan College of Mines. James' father spends his days telling C&H how to improve machines and get more work out of the men."

Suddenly everything made perfect sense, but all I could say was, "Oh."

Mr. Edwards put his hand gently on my back. "No matter what James thinks of this strike, or your family, he has no right to hurt you as he did. If he ever bothers you again, even with taunts, I want to know about it."

"Yes, sir. Thank you," I said.

He left then, and as I finished my dinner, I remembered something my father and Mr. Hakala told us last year. They said that one day, some "college boy name of Richards" had been down watching the two of them load tram cars. He watched and watched and finally asked if either of them understood English. "Little bit," my father had said.

I'm sure the man used proper English, but here is

how Papa told it. "You load rock fast, good. I want watch you so utter men do dat way."

Papa was not in a good mood that day, so he had said, "You want me load more fast? Pay better. I load real fast."

Richards is a very common name in Red Jacket. I did not realize it until tonight, but that man must have been James Richards' father.

Thursday, November 27

I know we celebrate Thanksgiving because the Pilgrims were thankful that they had enough food in a new land, but it is hard to think about being thankful this year. At the beginning of this strike, I wanted to get the arguing over with. Now I just wish the whole thing would end.

Another striking man is in the hospital today and might die. Papa told us he saw the whole thing from a little way off. Some men from the militia came very close to the WFM Hall on Sixth Street. Our men did not want them so close and started to beat up one of the guards. Papa said there was a lot of confusion and other soldiers fired shots to help the soldier who was beaten. I wonder if that soldier is thankful that somebody might die because he came too close to the Union Hall. I wonder if the man who was shot is thankful for anything.

I got to come home to be with my family for the day. Maude does not have any family, so she stayed to serve Mr. and Mrs. Edwards their Thanksgiving dinner. They had turkey and dressing and pumpkin pie. I think I know why they are thankful. I wonder if Maude is thankful for her job with them.

The meat from the buck Matti shot earlier this fall is all gone. All the other deer are hiding or somebody else shot them. Our dinner was a rabbit *mojakk*a and thimbleberry *marjavelia*. There was enough for one bowl for everyone, but no second helpings. There was nothing left over.

I am thankful that Papa stays away from danger at the parades and has not gotten hurt, even though the paper never printed his letter. I am thankful to be working and have plenty to eat, but I feel guilty that I eat so well while my family often goes hungry.

Mr. and Mrs. Edwards are very kind to me, and I have learned a lot about keeping house. Mrs. Edwards corrects my English sometimes, but my grammar has gotten better because of it. I have been able to keep up with my schooling, but sometimes I wonder, what is the point? Will I always be stuck working as a maid? I should be thankful, but sometimes I am not.

A lot of the snow has melted for the moment, but the ground is frozen and bare. The trees are gray. The houses are gray. The sky is gray. My heart feels gray and it is only the beginning of winter.

━━◆◆◆━━

"**F**oreign Agitators Must Be Driven From the District At Once."** That is what the headline of the *Daily Mining Gazette* in Houghton said. Newspapers are supposed to print news, but this newspaper seems to print only what the company wants it to say. When strikers were murdered in Seeberville, Sheriff Cruse did not rush to investigate, but now that three Cornish strike breakers got shot, everyone is searching.

Why do they blame everything on those of us who are Finnish? The Cornishmen always think they are better than we are just because they came here first. Oh, look at me. I am making no sense at all. What good is it to complain about others if I cannot keep my own mind straight?

Last Friday, Judge O'Brien had a final hearing for all the people who were arrested at the Allouez streetcar station for trying to keep scabs from going to work. He said they were guilty of contempt of court for going against his order not to harass men who wanted to work, but then he suspended their sentences. They didn't have to go to jail. On Saturday, the Citizen's Alliance people started yelling that Judge O'Brien should be voted out of office. They said what he did will make people even more violent.

Then around two in the morning Sunday, some men started shooting at two houses in Painesdale where Cornishmen who are strikebreakers were living. Three men got killed and a girl about my age was badly hurt. The Citizen's Alliance now says they were right, and we are on the edge of chaos. "It's time for this reign of terror to end," they say.

They had a big rally yesterday. They want Sheriff Cruse to crack down on our men and kick all the union people out of the area. More mass meetings are planned for Wednesday. All the businesses are going to close and give their workers time off, with pay, to go to these meetings. All the Finnish people are called "radicals" even though people from lots of other countries are on strike, too.

The WFM says it was not strikers who did the shooting. They say probably the Waddies did it to make the union look bad and that the Citizen's Alliance was only formed to do violence to our union men.

I think this will never be unmixed. Everybody wants an excuse to hate the other side. The one time lately that I managed to get to the library, Marie hurried away from me. She said she had to go straight home. The ladies who come to have tea with Mrs. Edwards always stop talking whenever I come into the parlor. I have to take back ways to go home on Saturday nights and to come back to work late Sunday evening. My heart aches. I am tired of crying myself to sleep at night.

At least nobody else got killed although lots more people have been in and out of the hospital. Papa read us the Finnish papers after dinner today. Wednesday, some 10,000 people crammed into the Armory and the Coliseum. Mr. Rees and Mr. Petermann, lawyers for C&H, were the ones who planned the meetings and spoke to the people. Papa and Mama both say this shows who is really running everything. They talked about how the citizens of the copper district should rise above the lawless union and show who is better.

La-di-da-da! That's how I feel right now. I want to be sassy at somebody so I know I am still worth something, even if it is wrong to be sassy.

Matti walked with me back to Mr. Edwards' house. "Emma, you mustn't take it so personal," he told me. "We know who we are. God knows how we really are. That's all that matters." I managed to bite back my tears.

Mr. Edwards was in the kitchen when I got there. He actually invited Matti in. "Please," he said, "You must come in and warm yourself before you walk home."

So Matti, Mr. Edwards and I sat at the kitchen table with cups of hot chocolate. Mr. Edwards looked at both of us and said, "These are hard times we are living through. Try not to listen too much to the loudest people on either side. Most of us, while we might not approve of the WFM, know that you miners have real grievances. My father once was where your father is now. We know how it is. We know you are good people."

Then we talked of school and how a good education will bring about better times. Mr. Edwards shook Matti's hand before he left.

Maude told me something else later. When I went up to our attic room, she said, "You know why Mr. Edwards is so fond of you, don't you?"

When I shook my head, she told me, "Mrs. Edwards had a stillborn baby who would be about your age if she had lived. God has not blessed them with another child."

Friday, December 19

———◆———

The days are so short this time of the year. It is dark until after breakfast, barely light when Mr. Edwards leaves for the store and dark again long before he gets home. The blackness pulls at my heart. I feel like I am in a deep cave.

Mr. MacNaughton had said the men had to return to work by today or their jobs would be given to others. There are still about 3,000 men on strike. But some businessmen managed to talk him into waiting until January first. That is not much to hope for. A grand jury has been called to investigate all the violence. They began to meet this week. There was even a bill introduced in the Congress in Washington, D.C., to try to get the company to agree to arbitrate. It did not pass.

Mrs. Edwards said I may help trim their Christmas tree tomorrow. We have never had a Christmas tree, even in good times. The Sunday after Thanksgiving, we sang a special hymn at church, *"Hoosianna, Daavidin poika."* It helps us remember that celebrating the birth of Jesus will come soon. *Tuomaanpäivä,* St. Thomas Day, when men's work is done, will start tomorrow, but no Christmas tree. "Too worldly," our pastor says, and my father agrees. I don't think I will tell my family about helping to decorate Mrs. Edwards' tree.

There is one bright little spark of light ahead though. Big Annie and some of the other women are planning a party for children at the Italian Hall on December 24. Papa said Mama can take us girls. Mr. Edwards says I may leave early that day to meet Mama and my sisters at the party. I can hardly wait.

—◆—

Thursday, December 25

It cannot be Christmas. It doesn't feel anything like it should. I wish yesterday were a horrid dream. I want to wake up, but I am awake.

Sunday, December 28

We buried most of them today. Maybe I am in that dark place, too. My head hurts so much I cannot think. I do not want to think.

Monday, December 29

I woke up crying again last night. Mama came in and held me close. Jenni and Katri did not even wake up. I don't know why. They were there, too. But they did not go to the funerals. Only Papa and I went because of my friend Lempi.

Tuesday, December 30

I sat at our bedroom window, staring out at the snow and the long shadows on the ground. I stared at the dark woods that I love in spring and summer, watching the dark night steal over everything. How I want to go away somewhere warm and light. I stared at my journal.

Papa came up, set down the oil lamp, and rubbed my back. He put a blanket around me. I had not realized

I was shivering. For a while he said nothing. Then we talked in Finnish.

"Why did you first start writing about the strike in your journal?" he asked me.

"I wanted to sort it all out," I said.

"Well, maybe if you sort this out, too, writing it there, it will quit hurting your head. Life goes on. You have to go on with it." He rubbed my back for a while longer. I wished he would put his arms around me like Mr. Edwards did when he came to see if I was all right, but that is not Papa's way of showing he loves me. Papa left the lamp next to me and handed me a newly sharpened pencil. Then he went back downstairs. I heard him tell everybody I could keep the lamp lit as long as I needed to and to leave me alone for a while, so I could sort things out.

I will really try now to put this down and find my *sisu* again.

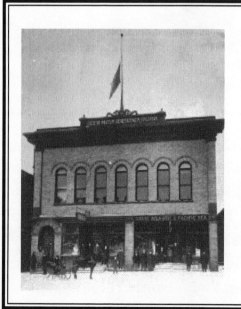

The front of the Italian Hall taken the day after the tragedy. The words on the top of the building say, "Societa Mutua Beneficenza Italiana" (Italian Mutual Benefit Society) The door way at the left with the stone arch led to the stairwell with the stairs up to the hall above where the arched windows are.
Photo MTU-N

The Christmas Party at the Italian hall started out so fine, so happy. The big room was crowded with smiling children, five or more children for every parent there. We had Papa's union book with us because we were told we would need it, but nobody asked to see it after all. Those stairs . . . About as wide as Papa is tall. Those stairs.

I hate those stairs!

The fatal staircase.
Photo SV-N

There was so much light in the middle of that afternoon. Everybody was smiling, bright as a summer day.

We sang Christmas songs in four languages. English, German, Finnish, and I'm not sure what the fourth was, maybe Italian since it was in the Italian Hall. There was a little Christmas tree, not much of one, and no candles on it. Just a bit of tinsel—a dime's worth I heard somebody say—and some pink and blue crepe paper, but it didn't matter. It was still pretty.

There were lots of people I knew and many more I didn't know. Lempi found me. I had not seen her in months, not since the church picnic I think. Still, she is . . . was my best friend before Marie and she helped me get over Mr. Hakala's death.

The saffron cake was so good. Bright yellow like the sun. Like the sun I need right now in the darkness of my mind. Lempi brought me a piece of it. We talked and talked. Jenni and Katri ran around, as much as there was room to in the crowded hall.

The hall got more and more crowded. There was not an empty chair anywhere in the rows and rows of folding chairs they had set up. Even the balcony area on the stairwell side (over the ticket office and restroom areas) was full of people.

<hr/>

The inside of the Italian Hall the day after the tragedy. *Photo MTU-N*

They decided not to do the Mother Goose Play they had practiced. Lots of children got anxious to see Santa Claus. They put a chair for Santa up on the stage by the Christmas tree. We were supposed to line up along the far wall and go up a few steps to the stage. After getting our presents, we were to go down the few steps on the other side of the stage and out into a narrow hallway by the restrooms. From that hall, we could go back into the party. Some families went on through the entryway and down **those** stairs to go home once they got their presents. They were the lucky ones.

Some children started pushing and shoving. Big Annie tried to get them all to sit down. Some did, but some didn't. Jenni, Katri and I were sort of in the middle of the line. Katri was so excited. I guided them along. Lempi was a little way ahead of us. Mama kept smiling at me while she talked with some of the women she knows from the Women's Auxiliary.

Finally, we got to the stage. Santa reached into his bag and gave Jenni and Katri each a doll. "I am too grown up for a doll," I told him, "but I do like candy." He smiled back and handed me a green scarf and mittens along with the candy.

"This will match that pretty green dress," he said.

That dress, my life, both keep changing colors—for the worse.

My white confirmation dress dyed green—well it matched the season anyway. After that day, Mama had to dye it black for the funerals.

———◆———

When we were at home later, we sat in the kitchen with Jaako and Matti. Papa had gone back to the Italian Hall with Mama after we got out.

"Somebody's knocking at the door," Katri said.

I went to see who. When I opened the door, there stood Mr. Edwards. He let out a huge sigh when he saw me. "Finally, the right house! Emma! Thank God you are all right." He wrapped his arms around me and hugged me. Then Jakko came out from the kitchen.

"I'm sorry to intrude in your home," Mr. Edwards told him. "I went down there to try and see. I kept hearing the name Niemi. I had to know. I've been all up and down this street calling your name. Someone finally pointed to this house."

Matti came out of the kitchen and shook Mr. Edwards' hand. "Thank you for the oranges. They were a real treat."

Mr. Edwards had given me a whole sack of oranges last Saturday.

I am avoiding it again. I must make myself back up.

We were still on the stage when we heard the cry. "Fire! Fire!"

People started screaming, running for the door. I grabbed Jenni and Katri.

People running for the doors tried to jump over rows of chairs. The last I saw of Lempi was the back of her coat as she disappeared into the crowd at the doors. Crashing chairs, falling tables. People yelling. Jenni and Katri crying for Mama. I looked for her. I grabbed my sisters, held their hands tightly, and jumped from the stage.

My heart was pounding. I didn't know whether to run or stay. Jenni and Katri were screaming and pulling at my dress. Then suddenly, Mama was near us.

"I don't smell no smoke," she said. "You stay *right here* or I'll thrash you. I'm going to look around." Katri buried her head in my chest. Jenni clung to my shoulders. I put my arms around both of them.

Early in the party, Mrs. Sizer had been playing the piano when we sang Christmas carols. She was trying to play it again, trying to calm people down. Big Annie kept yelling out, telling people to sit down, that there was no fire.

The screaming and crashing still sound in my head. The mishmash of faces, people running, arms waving . . . jamming against one another at the doors, pushing and shoving and pushing, and pushing . . . I saw a little girl fall. Others rushed right over her trying to get out. Katri and Jenni were hugging me and they did not see. Maybe that's why . . .

I felt someone grab my shoulder. "Emma!" It was Mama. "Can't get out the main doors. Too crowded. Come this way."

She led us along the edge of the stage, through the doors we were supposed to use after getting our presents, into the vestibule, and down that hall to the back of the building. There was a fire escape at the end.

I don't remember climbing down, but I must have. A lot of other people followed us.

The yelling and screaming in the street in front were worse than what we had heard up in the hall. Men and women who had sent their children with friends or relatives tried to get in. Firemen arrived to find there was no fire. Deputies came with batons thinking there was another riot.

"Emma, stay close behind me," Mama said. But I lagged behind. I wanted to see if Lempi was out in the street. I caught sight of the stairs. People were piled upon people, all in a huge jumble. Like a stack of wood piled too high and toppled over. I couldn't see Lempi anywhere.

The things people were yelling!

"They're trying to kill us all!"

"Deputies won't let people out!"

"They blocked the doors!"

I put my hands over my ears to shut out the screaming and ran to catch up with Mama and my sisters. Somehow, that green scarf had wound itself around my head, and neck and I saw I was wearing the mittens.

Once we got home, Mama left again with Papa to go back and see if they could help in any way and to help Lempi's parents find her. A long time later, they still weren't back. Jaako made us some hot milk. That was when Mr. Edwards came.

I started to sip my milk and then said, "Why do we still have milk? Isn't it time for Daisy to freshen before her calf is born?"

We usually stop milking Daisy two months before her calf is born, and we wait a few weeks afterward to make sure the calf has enough. Then we use the milk the calf doesn't need. After the calf is weaned, we have plenty of milk again.

"Yeah," Jaako said. "It's hard on her, but we need the milk. Everybody in this family gave up something. Daisy got to do her part, too."

Why did I even care about milk, or no milk, right then?

Firemen and other people could not get all those crushed people out at the bottom of the stairs. They had to go up the fire escape the way we came out and untangle people from the top down, just like you have to untangle a fallen woodpile from the top down. Mama and Papa helped carry the some of the bodies from the Italian Hall to the Red Jacket Town Hall a block away, so parents could come and look for their children. Fifty-eight children were trampled and crushed to death in the stairwell. My friend Lempi was one of them. Fifteen adults died, too.

———◆———

The Coroner's Inquest started today. Even some children my age testified about what they saw or didn't see. Nobody agrees on anything. Big Annie was sure the man who yelled "Fire!" had a Citizen's Alliance button on. But later, she wasn't really sure. Other people said they saw it, too. But others could not even agree on what he looked like, or if they saw the same person, or anything. Maybe that is not so hard to understand. I know I heard the cry, but I could not see who it was. Now, I don't even **want** to remember. I want to forget it all, make it go away.

My head is not hurting as much now, so maybe Papa was right. I have to get it out.

Horrible rumors are still going around. Nobody is acting very Christian, or like it was the time to celebrate Jesus' birth.

There is no Peace on Earth in Calumet.

Somebody said there really was a fire in the Christmas tree. I was right there. I **know** that was not true. Mr. MacNaughton said in the paper that it was a horrible tragedy. He offered money to the families. In anger, they refused.

Mr. Moyer said it was all the company's fault. He blamed the Citizen's Alliance. He was not even there. How could he know?

That doesn't excuse what they did to him. The day after Christmas, Sheriff Cruse went to see Mr. Moyer at his hotel room in Hancock. He said he could not protect him any more if he didn't take back what he said about the Citizen's Alliance. Mr. Moyer told Sheriff Cruse to get out. Right after he left, a bunch of men came and beat up Mr. Moyer. They kicked him and shot him in the back and then dragged him to the train station. They threw him on the train to Chicago!

Sheriff Cruse has not started to investigate that, yet.

It takes a long time to have that many funerals— mostly on the same day. They were spread out among five different churches. Papa and I walked together to our church. We sat as close as we could to Lempi's family. I just stared at the floor the whole time. I could not make myself look at Lempi's coffin or the coffins of the others who had been members of our church. Papa took my hand as the procession from our church joined the others in going to Lake View Cemetery.

Mr. Moyer survived on the train to Chicago. At least we weren't burying him, too.

Thousands of people walked in the procession to the cemetery. They dug two huge graves for all the coffins: one big one for all the Catholics and another for Protestants. I saw a few single graves, too. I guess some people wanted their own. I like to think Lempi is not lonely where she is with the others.

Inside one of the churches at the funerals (most likely the Finnish Church). *Photo MTU-N*

God sent fresh snow. Everything was pretty with a clean white blanket, but the black, half-frozen earth around those coffins will never be clean and pure for me. I wish I had another agate for Lempi.

Church bells tolled all day long. There was even a special train bringing 500 men from the iron range around Negaunee and Ishpeming. Four union men carried each white casket with a child in it. Somebody got flowers from somewhere—certainly not this frozen north—to put on top of each casket. Horse-drawn hearses, other coffins on sleds . . . a brass band played as we walked. A whole bunch of Cornish miners (they were pretty nice about it, considering most of them are not on strike) sang "Jesus, Lover of My Soul," and "Rock of Ages."

Big Annie was at the front carrying the flag. Tears streamed down her face. I did not have any tears left.

Trenches with coffins at Lake View Cemetery. *Photo MTU-N*

I could not make myself sing. I stared ahead of me or at the ground. How I wanted Papa to put his arms around me. I wanted to be a little girl again and crawl into his lap, bury my face in his strong chest. I put my arms around him once, but he was stiff. His stiff hand did fall onto my shoulder after they covered the coffins with dirt.

It must have been really hard to dig that frozen ground. Lots of times if somebody dies in winter, they have to store the coffin someplace in the cold, which is never a problem, and wait until spring to bury it.

It was dark when we got home. The stars seemed especially bright. I could even see Orion's belt and his hand on his shield.

I can see the stars now, too. I think I will turn off the lamp and count out seventy-three stars or maybe more. People keep arguing about exactly how many died. I will count Polaris, the North Star, for Lempi.

Thursday, January 1, 1914

Last year on New Year's Eve, when we were on our way back from sauna, Mr. Hakala said he did not believe in tossing the *vihta* to see what the New Year would bring. Papa told him to go ahead just for fun. So Mr. Hakala did, but he picked it up right away and said, "It's all foolishness anyway."

I saw it was pointed toward the graveyard, and that is where Mr. Hakala ended up.

Last night as we got ready to toss them, Papa said the same thing he does every year, "Better not point to a church. None of you, not even Jaako and Matti, are old enough to get married."

Nobody's pointed to the graveyard or a church. Nothing good, nothing bad. I think I will like a year like that.

The melted tin told a different story. Papa melted the pieces of tin and each of us poured a tiny ladle full into cold water. When the hissing stopped, Papa pulled out the piece, looked at it carefully against the lantern light, and told us what shape he thought it looked like.

Last year, mine looked like animals—the sign for true friends. Now one of my true friends is dead and the other is not allowed to speak to me. Papa's tin broke into pieces last year, but he said each piece looked rough and spotty, so he must be going to get a lot of money. I know a broken piece means bad luck.

This year, mine was a bird. I could sure use some good luck. Papa laughed when his stayed together and told of money again. Jaako's was a flower. We teased him about which of the girls in Swedetown had her eyes on him. Jenni and Katri both had horses, and Matti's looked like a ship.

"Where would you like to go?" Mama asked, because both horses and ships mean the person will take a trip. Jenni said it would be fun to ride the train to Freda Park next summer. Katri said she wanted to take the street car to Houghton.

"Back out to Mr. Lamppa's is the only place I'll be going," Matti said.

Mama's was last. Hers looked like a wreath. "Well, an end to this strike would certainly be something to celebrate," she said.

I was supposed to go back to Mr. Edwards' house this evening, but the snow was coming down too hard, so I will wait until early morning.

Maybe getting back to work will keep my mind so busy I won't have any dreams at all. I hope so. What will he think if I wake up screaming like I have at home?

Saturday, January 3

———◆———

It felt good to be back in Mr. Edwards' house filled with electric lights to chase away all the dark shadows. Even though I only worked two days, he handed me my full pay for the week and last week, too.

"I haven't earned all this," I said.

Mr. Edwards closed my hand around the money and said, "Yes, you have."

I saw Mama wipe away a tear when I gave it to her.

———◆———

Sunday, January 11

Usually I like January. One year Papa made us skis out of old barrel stays. (Stays are the long slats of wood that go up and down the sides of a barrel.) We skied down our hill, struggled to climb back up, and skied down again, laughing all the way. Lots of children often slide down on pieces of cardboard. The ponds and lakes are frozen so thick we do not have to worry about falling through the ice when we take a short cut across or want to slide and skate. There are always snowball fights in the field. Papa, Jaako and Matti talk on and on about who will win each hockey game.

This year, I hate January. The nights seem endless, and the days are cold and gray. Katri begged me to join them sliding down our hill, but I said I had to study for my exams. I said the same thing when some of my old classmates asked me to come out to the pasture for a snowball fight. I sat at the upstairs window and watched them. My reading book was open, but I never turned a page.

Right before I left to walk back to Mr. Edwards' house, I went out to the shed to say hello to Daisy. I rubbed her nose and patted her belly. "The next time I see you, you might have your new calf," I whispered. "I'm sorry Jenni has to keep milking you this time. You probably wonder why we have not let you freshen like we always did. The truth is there's not a whole lot for our family to eat without your milk, so thank you."

Fifth Street in Red Jacket (Calumet) in winter. Note the show shoes, and that sleigh runners have replaced wheels on the wagon and the depth of the piles of snow. *Photo MTU-N*

I thought back to last April when Matti walked half way to Electric Park to a farm with a good bull. Papa bought Daisy from that farm, and we have sent her back there every April since she was old enough to breed. The calf always goes back when it is able to leave Daisy. Our shed is too small for more than one cow. One year, the farmer keeps the calf as payment for the bull's service. The next year, Papa gets to keep it. The farmer has the use of ours until Papa has his farm. He has one other cow so far.

I hope this year Daisy has a bull. Papa will trade it for one who is not related to Daisy. Then our farm will have a bull to keep building Papa's dairy herd.

I dragged my feet on the walk back to Laurium.

⚊◆⚊

Wednesday, January 14

I have stopped reading the newspapers. People say Mr. MacNaughton left for a vacation, but he really went to Boston to meet with the company owners. They say people are leaving the area by the thousands. The train is full every time it heads south and nearly empty when it comes back. They say that more people are working for C&H now than there were before the strike started. They must not be very good because not as much rock is coming out of the mines.

They say Mr. Moyer recovered from his injuries and is back up here. They say that a big New York newspaper said Houghton County is not a community of American citizens, but one of aliens brought here from other countries to slave for a monopoly ruled by Boston.

Mrs. Edwards sent me on some errands today and I did not even stop at the library. I happened to see Big Annie on the street. They say her husband left her while she was spending ten days in jail for the assault charge and that she went home to a cold, empty house. Her eyes were dull and her face long. She walked with her shoulders rounded and did not seem so tall. She did not recognize me when I said, "Hello."

Almost all the National Guard men have left. They finally turned off the huge search light, "MacNaughton's Eye," which has shown over the mine offices for so long. It is even darker at night. I should study for my exams, but I do not care anymore.

—————◆————

Sunday, January 25

D aisy has a fine, healthy bull. Everybody was happy about that since this is Papa's year to keep her offspring.

This afternoon Jenni and Katri asked Papa to let them jump out of our bedroom window into the snow. Papa said they could, and they ran off laughing to bundle up in warm clothes. "You, too, Emma," he said. "Go have a bit of fun."

"I'm too tired," I said.

"No, you're not. You slept in church. Go with your sisters, now."

Last year I was just as excited as they were when the snow got deep enough to jump out the window. The blast of cold air and the drop usually grab at my heart and lungs in a way that is both frightening and exciting. This year all I felt was a soft thud. I forced myself to grin for Jenni and Katri.

Wednesday, January 28, *(I think)*

———◆———

Somehow, I managed to pass my seventh grade reading and math exams. When Papa saw my C's, he put his hands on my shoulders and said in Finnish, "I am still proud because you stayed in school. I know you will do better again when you can go back to school in the day." This semester of night school I am taking history and science.

A while back, a grand jury indicted Mr. Moyer and many other WFM members for conspiring to keep men from going to work. The men who beat up Mr. Moyer were not charged with any crime.

They say Mr. Moyer tried to get workers all over Michigan to join in a sympathy strike. It probably will not happen. But the House of Representatives in Washington, D.C., voted to send some people up here to investigate.

I only nodded when Mr. Edwards handed me today's paper. He put his finger under my chin and lifted it so I looked at him. "Emma, where's your smile?" he asked.

I felt my lip quiver. I only shrugged my shoulders because I thought I might cry again if I tried to talk. "Maybe I should send you to see my doctor," he said.

I bit the inside of my cheek to get control of myself and managed to say, "No thank you, sir, I am not sick."

<hr/>

Thursday, February 5

L ast night I dreamed I was at the Christmas Party again and woke up screaming. Maude turned on the light and came around the curtain to my side of our room. She hugged me for a while, and we talked.

"I think I am going crazy," I told her.

"No, you aren't, Emma," she said.

Then she told me about something that happened to her. She was six years old and the only child in her family. Her parents had a farm out near Gratiot Lake. Her father liked to ice fish in the winter and even had a little shed he would drag out onto the ice. It was late in the winter the day it happened. Her mother went out to the ice fishing shed to take her father a jug of hot coffee. There were little slushy puddles on top of the ice, but her father had said the ice was still strong. Well, her mother slipped and fell. When she hit the ice there was a terrible cracking sound. The ice broke all apart and both her parents and the shed went down into the dark water. They never came up. Maude had been standing on the shore the whole time. She saw it all.

"I was all alone and had to run almost two miles to the nearest neighbor for help," she told me. "Those same neighbors took me in and raised me. I had nightmares for months afterward. Some people said they should send me to an asylum. My adoptive mother told them I only needed lots of love. She always told me to think about blueberry pie because it's good and sweet and happy."

She hugged me again. "I still think about blueberry pie whenever I'm sad."

"When I think of blueberry pie, I think about how much work it is to pick that many berries," I said.

"Then what's the happiest thing you can think of?"

"Picking daisies on a warm day in June. I even named our cow Daisy because of that. We got her when I was eight. Mama said she would be mine to care for, so I could name her."

"Whenever you are afraid, or sad, think about picking daisies."

So I went back to sleep thinking about a field so full of daisies it looked like a white quilt with tiny yellow polka dots for the daisy centers.

———◆◆◆———

It was so odd, what happened in the back room of Mr. Edwards' store today. I was back there sorting out potatoes again when suddenly the room seemed to disappear, and I saw the open graves again. I felt like I was being dragged down into them. I gripped my chest and said, "Daisies, daisies," over and over. I must have said it pretty loud. When Mr. Edwards put his hand on my shoulder, I jumped.

"Emma, are you all right?" he asked.

My heart was still pounding. I could hardly catch my breath. I could not stand it any more and burst into tears. It was a good thing there were no customers at the time. Mr. Edwards put his arms around me and rubbed my back. It felt so good. I cried on his chest for the longest time. I told him about all the dreams I have had and what Maude said, and everything I was afraid to say before.

"Am I crazy?" I asked him.

"If you were, I don't think you would be able to tell me about all this so easily," he said. He brushed my hair back. "Blueberries and daisies. Maude is a wise woman. I think you should keep following her advice. Emma, you are a very bright, strong young woman. I think God has a good plan for you."

Monday, February 16

The congressional hearings have been going on for a week now. So far, there is nothing in the papers that I have not read before. In my history class, we are reading about the men who wrote the Constitution. They had a lot of arguments, but they managed to come together about it. I wonder if they thought back then that they were making history. I wonder if we are making history here and now. I wonder if the congressmen will be able to help us come together with C&H. Will anyone ever study about us?

A jury found four of the company men involved in the murders at Seeberville guilty of manslaughter. Three of them got the minimum sentence of seven to fifteen years in prison. The fourth was found "not guilty." Our men say they got off too easy. Others say they should all have been found "not guilty" because they were just doing their jobs. I do not know what I think anymore.

Friday, February 20

Maude is always the one who serves dinner when Mr. and Mrs. Edwards have guests, but today she went to bed in the middle of the afternoon with chills and fever. I have often served tea to Mrs. Edwards and the ladies, but I began to panic, mostly because tonight's guests were Mr. and Mrs. Richards, James and his younger sister.

Mrs. Edwards came out to the kitchen to help put the finishing touches on the dinner before they arrived. She must have seen my hands shaking.

"I'm very confident in you, Emma," she said. "These are our close friends, so it isn't so formal. Don't you let young James rattle you. I'm going to serve family style, so you will only have to put the serving dishes on the table. Stand by the sideboard in case we need anything. Serve the coffee and dessert just as you do tea."

Daisies, daisies, daisies, I said to myself as I went to open the front door. Mr. Richards handed me his coat and hat without even looking at me. James glared, and I ignored him. Mrs. Richards smiled and thanked me for helping her with her cape. Miss Rose said, "Hello, Emma," as she took off her coat. I had met her once on the playground at school. I hung their wraps in the front closet while they went to the parlor.

I put everything on the table and announced dinner. Mr. and Mrs. Edwards sat at the ends of the table with Mr. Richards and James on one side, Mrs. Richards and Rose on the other. James was closer to Mrs. Edwards.

Everything went fine through the meal. But every time I needed to go around to James' side of the table, he would put his foot out so I had to go around it. Mr. Richards kept looking at me with his brow wrinkled. Many people say I look like my father, so I tried not to look right at him.

The strike came up close to the end of the meal. Mr. Richards was complaining about some of the replacement workers. "They just don't work as hard as those Finns." He stopped and looked right at me.

Mrs. Edwards spoke quickly, "And wasn't it nice to see the sun out so bright yesterday? I'm beginning to long for spring break-up."

Then Mr. Edwards brought up the latest hockey game. I wished some magic from the stories of my childhood could make me invisible, but all I could do was stand quietly by the sideboard.

"Emma, I think we're ready for coffee and desert," Mrs. Edwards finally said.

As I turned, I heard Mr. Richards say, "Her father is one of those strikers, isn't he?"

Their voices carried into the kitchen.

"Yeah, he is," I heard James say.

"James, mind your manners." That was Mrs. Richards.

"Chester, why in the world have you got one of them working for you?"

I began to feel very hot, and it wasn't from the stove or the pot of coffee. I walked out of the kitchen carrying three plates of chocolate cake and gritting my teeth. There was an awkward silence. I managed to give the ladies their dessert. Then I heard a buzz of whispers and "sh, sh," as I came in with the other three plates. James had his foot out farther this time. I set his cake in front of him with shaking hands. Mr. Edwards was tapping his fingers on the table.

I left again to get the coffee pot. Anger boiled inside me. Our pastor's words from last Sunday came back to me: "Jesus told them, if the soldiers force you to carry a burden one mile, carry it two." I thought about daisies again, picked up the pot and went back to the dining room.

I poured Mrs. Richards' coffee first and then Mrs. Edwards'. James' foot was way out, right where I would have to step. Oh, how I wanted to touch it with mine and then pour that scalding coffee right in his snooty lap. Instead, I stopped still and said, "Excuse me, Mr. Richards," using his last name like I would for his father, "Might you please move your foot back under the table? I would not want to trip and spill this hot coffee all over you by accident." Then I took an unusually large step over his out-stretched leg and went on around and filled his father's cup.

Mrs. Edwards covered her mouth to hide a smile. Mr. and Mrs. Richards' mouths dropped open. Mr. Edwards' eyes had a twinkle in them by the time I filled his cup. Then, with my head high, I returned to my place at the sideboard.

Mr. Edwards finally broke the silence. "John, do you remember when we were children growing up in Central? Remember how we used to walk by the mine captain's house on our way to play in the woods? Do you remember what you always said?"

"Goodness, no. That was ages ago."

"Well, I'll remind you. You always said, 'Someday, I'm going to have a house like that with lace in the windows, and my wife won't have to scrub floors.' That is what our parents wanted for us. Is what you want for your children, any different than what 'those Finns,' as you call them, want for their wives and children? Do you know what my biggest problem with this strike is?"

"I can't imagine," Mr. Richards said.

"My problem is figuring out a way to keep Emma working for me when it finally ends, and then later, how to let her go when something better for her comes along, and it will come along. This young lady has more brains than a few others in this room. She can speak in Finnish to some of my customers, and perfect English to me in the next sentence. Then she tells the customer an estimate of the total for her groceries. When I add it up, she's right almost to the penny! We must all, every single one of us, never forget our humble beginnings."

It fell silent again.

Finally, Mr. Richards cleared his throat and said, "Chester, you and I have never felt the same politically, so let's leave it at that. Delicious cake, Jessie." He put another forkful in his mouth.

I'll never have to think about daisies again. I'll just remember what Mr. Edwards said about me tonight.

⸻◆⸻

Thursday, February 26

Mrs. Edwards sent me out to do the errands this afternoon just in time for me to get over to the train station to watch Big Annie leave on a lecture tour. She will go all over the country and talk to people, asking them to give money to support the strike. The ladies gave her a fancy feathered hat. She told everybody, "Of course we would rather die than give up." She smiled, but there was a look about her that gave me the feeling it was not a real smile.

Later when I came out of the Post Office, I saw Marie on her way home from school. I called out to her. It has been so long. She came running up to me, and we hugged each other. I told her how I have been doing and asked how school was going for her.

"It goes all right, but I wish you help me with English," she said.

"Does your father still say we cannot see each other?"

"He hasn't said much since Christmas Eve, and, well, you know," she said almost in a whisper.

"Do you think it would be a good idea to ask him if we could meet, so I could help you with your school work?"

"I don't know. Maybe if I try Saturday after he goes to Confession. He might be more likely to say it is all right then. Do you still go to the Library?"

"Sometimes. I'll ask if I can go next Friday afternoon," I said.

"Well, I'll ask my father this Saturday. Then I'll tell you next Friday what he says."

We went our separate ways. I am going to pray very hard in church this Sunday. But now I had better study for my history test. I want to bring up my grades.

Sunday, March 1

Why is it that every time I begin to feel hopeful, things go badly again? Sheriff Cruse announced in the newspaper yesterday that John Huhta, a Finnish miner in Painesdale and the corresponding secretary for the South Range local WFM, confessed to the murder of the two Cornish miners last December. The paper said he had been drinking a lot lately and feeling bad. He handed a bullet shell to a deputy and told him, "I got this souvenir for you; it is the one I took with me on the night we did the Painesdale job," the paper said.

So, all the talk is against us again. I am very sad that it turned out to be one of us. Papa was quiet at Sunday dinner. But he did say this, "At least he got it out, took the blame for what he done. Waddies at Seeberville never done that."

Mama nodded her head.

Matti cheered us all up by saying that he mastered shoeing horses and is learning to mend tools now. Early in January, he had told Papa he wanted to switch from academic classes at the high school to the trade center. He said if he is a skilled blacksmith when we have our farm, we won't have to pay someone else for those services. Now he says he can even do them for other farmers near us and maybe earn a little extra.

Friday, March 6

I made it to the library right about the time school would be letting out. I settled down with several newspapers to wait for Marie. This is the last week for the congressional hearings. The WFM gave testimony for the first three weeks. This week it has been C&H's turn. The company even took the representatives on an underground tour. MacNaughton did a good job convincing them that workers here have it good compared to places like Pennsylvania. It doesn't look like they will be able to end the strike by saying that C&H broke any labor laws. It surprised me to read that the company did admit some captains and managers are unfair.

When Marie came into the reading room, she had a smile on her face. "Papá said we might as well be friends out in the open since nothing he did stopped us anyway."

We worked on her English homework for a while, and then I had to leave. Mrs. Edwards always expects me to return from my errand trips by 4:30 PM so I can help Maude begin supper. I am going to ask Mrs. Edwards if it is all right for Marie to come by

after supper the nights I do not have classes. Maybe
she will let us work in the kitchen as long as I finish
the supper dishes.

———————

Wednesday, March 11

Mrs. Edwards said Marie may come to the back door, and we may work in the kitchen. I have classes on Tuesdays and Thursdays, so she came Monday and tonight. While I wash and dry the supper dishes, she reads her English homework aloud and I tell her what to correct. I've also been helping her learn new words. We are starting with everything in the kitchen. I make her practice saying sentences with the names of things and how they are used.

After an hour or so, Marie goes home and I go to my attic room to study my own homework. I have pulled my grades back up to B's. If I work harder, I still have time to make A's by the end of the school year.

Things are pretty quiet with the strike. The congressional committee went to Chicago to get Mr. Moyer's testimony. He said the men can end the strike any time they want to by having a referendum. It seems the union has given up trying to win. The company has already given men still working a small pay increase and a shorter day. The men get fifty cents more a day, but they work five and a half fewer hours each week, so they don't end up making much more than they did before the strike started. I understood from what Mr. Moyer said that the goal now is only to make sure our men can return to work without being punished.

Sunday, March 15

Papa and Jaako are quiet about the strike these days. I guess they still go to the meetings. Some of the men still say they will fight it out forever, but mostly they want to go back to work. Nobody says so out loud, but they are worried about the backlash that might happen when they do return.

Papa always asks how school is going for me. "You keep study," he always says, "Dats da only way you get ahead." Sometimes he asks me if he says things right, but it seems disrespectful to correct him.

For the first time in months, the strike is not on the front page of the newspapers. That is fine with me. I've only been reading the headlines, anyway. I need more time to study.

Saturday, March 28

————◆————

Sunshine streaming in the window wakes me up now. The streets are full of mud and slush. Every morning the puddles are frozen, but by noon water runs along the edges of the streets in little rivers. The snow has melted from around the sides of Mr. Edwards' house. Little green spikes are poking up through the wet, black dirt. Maude says they are crocuses and tulips. Spring flowers. I like that thought.

————◆————

Wednesday, April 1

Our men have been marching peacefully, and there had been no arrests for awhile. Then some men had a fight in a street in Red Jacket and a WFM member from Wolverine got shot. We were all hoping something might happen to make the company recognize the union. I do not think that will ever happen now.

Something strange happened, too. A lot of rumblings, like a little earthquake, happened over in Hancock. Dishes rattled in people's houses. The strike breakers all ran out of the Quincy mine and refused to work. The headline in the *Miners Magazine* said, "God Takes a Hand."

Last Sunday, I overheard Papa tell Mama that the bills are piling up for the union. He told Mama all is probably lost. The union is working to make sure men like Papa can go back to work without the strike being held against them.

I kept my nose in my science book, and memorized things I need to know for my next test, so Mama and Papa would not think I was listening to them.

Thursday, April 9

⟞⟝

Papa came to the back door of Mr. Edwards' house after the union meeting today and asked to see me. "WFM say no more money. Dey cut strike benefit," he said.

I didn't know what to say. I don't think Papa did, either. He stared at the kitchen floor and finally said, "You tink Mr. Edwards want you keep work a bit more?"

"Yes, I think so," I told Papa.

"Just tru summer. Den you go back to school right." He put his hands on my shoulders. "You promise?"

"I promise I will go back to regular school in the fall," I said.

⟞⟝

April 12, Easter Sunday

Christmas did not feel like Christmas, and Easter has turned out almost as bad. After church today, Papa and Jaako went to the union meeting to vote. A lot of the men wanted to keep up the fight. Papa and Jaako voted to end it. Now I wait and wonder if they will be allowed to go back to work.

When I got back to Mr. Edwards' house, it was still light enough to see that the crocuses have finally bloomed. At least there is something good in this world.

Tuesday, April 14

W ell, it's over.

The paper said that in the Calumet unit there were more votes to stay on strike, but across the whole copper district, most men voted to end it.

The papers say we should put it behind us now and move forward—forgive and forget. As much as some people hated us, and as angry as some men got, I don't think that will be easy. Union officials said in the papers that the strike was a glorious victory for workers everywhere. Newspapers all over the country read about us. Our nation's lawmakers have a better idea about how hard it is for working men.

It seems to me that families like ours went through a lot of misery for nothing. Well, not quite nothing. The men do have a shorter work day and a little bit more pay. I sat down with a pencil and figured up how much our family would have made if Papa and Jaako had not gone on strike. It would take several years with the little increase in pay to earn back what they lost since last July. That's if nothing we need to buy goes up in price.

Sunday, April 19

J enni was the one to tell me how it was at home last week. She asked me to come out with her to milk Daisy. First, she told me Papa said lots of the union men feel betrayed. The union promised to support us until we won, and they didn't.

"Papa and Jaako walked tall when they left the house to go turn in their union books and see if C&H would take them back," Jenni said. "They never got in any trouble the whole time, so they had a good chance."

"That's good. So when will they start?"

"That's the strange part," Jenni said. "Lots of men were told there are no jobs available. When Papa came home, he said the captain told him some man named Richards put in a good word for him and Jaako. They start work tomorrow."

I wondered if what Mr. Edwards said the night the Richards family came to dinner had something to do with it, but I did not say anything.

Sunday, April 26

Papa walked me back to Mr. Edwards' house this evening. I was surprised when Mr. Edwards greeted us and asked Papa to come in for a few minutes. We sat down at the kitchen table.

"Mr. Niemi, Emma is a good worker and a very bright young woman. Would you let her keep working for me through the summer and maybe beyond that?"

"Ya, she can keep work for summer, but she got to go school come fall."

Mr. Edwards explained his plan. I was so amazed at what he said that it was hard to translate so Papa could understand. In the fall, Mr. Edwards wants me to keep living at his house during the week. I will do morning chores before school. After school, I will serve tea and supper and do housework until 8 PM. Then I must study. The housework will pay my room and board. I will work at the store all day Saturday for one dollar.

Papa's eyes about popped out when he heard $1.00.

"Believe me," Mr. Edwards said, "your daughter is worth what she will earn."

He also told Papa he wants me to open a bank account to save some of my earnings. "I think she should go farther than high school," he told Papa. "I know people who could help her get a scholarship for college."

He also said that when Papa gets his land and my family moves onto it, he will make sure I go to the Finnish Church. If I serve Sunday dinner and do that bit of washing up, at the end of each month I can take the trolley to Lake Linden at noon on Friday. Papa will pick me up and take me home for the weekend. I would not have to come back until noon on Monday.

"You good man, Mr. Edwards. Emma can keep work for you dat way."

Papa and Mr. Edwards shook hands. I wished I could hug both of them, but that would not be proper. I have not felt this happy in a very long time.

⟢⟡⟣

Friday, May 1

M y afternoon errands took me past one of the schools today. A group of children twirled their ribbons in the May Pole dance. I stopped to watch and thought about everything that has happened since Marie and I danced last year.

May Day festivities, 1914. *Photo KNHP-Foster*

There has been so much hate and anger, so much

sorrow, so much death. It has been the darkest year of my life. On this, my thirteenth birthday, I have more hope than I ever had before. People say thirteen is an unlucky number. Twelve was my unlucky number. Thirteen has to be better.

When I got back to the house, I went around to the flower beds and picked a few daffodils. I put them in a vase on the tray when I took Mrs. Edwards her tea. I felt as bright and sunny as the flowers.

I have a chance to go to college if I work hard. Maybe I could go to Marquette Normal School and become a teacher. Maybe I could go to nursing school. I'm going to be somebody. I will do it for Lempi and all the other children who never can. I will do it for my family and myself. I will do it because I have *sisu*.

—◆—

Appendices

Area Map

Map Legend

1. Seeberville
2. Painesdale
3. Trimountain
4. South Range
5. Atlantic Mine
6. Houghton
7. Hancock, Quincy Mine
8. Boston Location
   (*near Electric Park*)
9. Swedetown
10. Red Jacket (Calumet)
11. Laurium
12. Lake Linden
13. Hubbell/ Tamarack City
14. Kearsarge
15. Allouez
16. Mohawk
17. Phoenix
18. Eagle River
19. Eagle Harbor
20. Copper Harbor
21. Central
22. Gay Stamp Mill
23. Trap Rock River Valley
24. Portage Lake Ship Canal Entry
25. Portage Lake Ship Canal
26. Jacobsville
27. Freda
28. Gratiot Lake

Modern highways, US 41 and M 26 somewhat follow the older railroad and trolley lines. Distances are approximately: 11 miles from Houghton to Lake Linden; 4 miles from Lake Linden to Calumet; 100 miles from Houghton to Marquette; 430 miles from Houghton to Chicago; 495 miles from Houghton to Lansing by modern road. In 1913, there was no bridge over the Straights of Mackinaw between the Michigan's Upper and Lower Peninsulas. Travel between Houghton and Lansing would have been by train from Houghton to Chicago and then to Lansing. A forty-minute brisk walk will take a person from Swedetown to Laurium.

Glossary

General meaning of Finnish
words and phrases used throughout the story.
Special thanks to Jim Kurtti

Ei yhtään—never

Hoosianna, Daavidin poika—a Finnish hymn sung during Advent, the four weeks before Christmas

Iisakinpäivä—Isaac's name day, the day a child is baptized (St. Isaac's Day)

Juustoa—oven cheese, sometimes called "squeaky cheese"

Karjala—to Finns, it means the particular region between Finland and Russia, the land of the Kalevala

The Kalevala—Finland's national epic poetry

Korppua—cinnamon toast

Lauta, lautat in plural—cedar benches in a sauna

Lölyä, or löylyä—steam

Marjavelia—literally, fruit soup, a fruit sauce served on something or eaten alone

Minä olen vain vuokralainen ja MacNaughton omistaa kartanon—I am still just a tenant and MacNaughton owns the manor.

Mojakka—stew

Osuuskauppa—cooperative, a business owned by its members

Raha—money

Rovasti—a clerical or religious position in the state church

Sisu—no exact translation, the quality some people have of cour-

age, determination or perseverance to survive life's greatest
challenges; the characteristic that takes over when determination and fortitude are gone.

Soumea puhutaan—Finnish is spoken here

Tuomaanpäivä—St. Thomas Day, a Finnish holiday just before
Christmas, when men's work (such as logging) was finished

Vihta—a small cedar or birch bough soaked in hot water

Vanhapojan kääntiä—pink and white peppermint candies (bach-
elor's candies) sold at the co-op stores

Viiliä—yogurt-like clabbered milk

Historical notes about the "Copper Country"

While most people know about the western frontier, fewer people know that the United States also had a northern frontier. A few years before the California gold rush, the United States Mineral Land Agency began leasing tracts of land in the Keweenaw Peninsula of Upper Michigan for copper mining. Explorers and others hoping to make fortunes headed for this region, known only to the Ojibwa people and a few French-Canadian fur trappers. Many of the first prospectors didn't make it through the harsh winters. Those who stayed needed to find money to build shaft houses and buy expensive machines to bring copper to the surface. They had to ship it across Lake Superior and down Lake Huron to Detroit and the rest of the world.

Experienced tin miners from Cornwall, England, immigrated to the area with their families. Soon loggers, farmers and businessmen moved to newly created towns. Between 1850 and 1860, the population in the region rose by more than 13,000.

A canal with locks was built around the rapids of the St. Mary's River at Sault Ste. Marie, connecting Lake Superior and Lake Huron. Ships could then go directly from one lake to the other instead of unloading, carrying supplies around the rapids and re-loading at the lower end. Another canal was dredged from Lake Superior into Portage Lake so ships could load and unload in calm water since Lake Superior often had violent storms. Mining moved from Keweenaw County south to Houghton County. A ferry carried people and goods between the new towns of Houghton, on the south side of a narrow arm of Portage Lake, and Hancock on the north. The first bridge between these twin towns was built in 1872.

"Calumet" consisted of a few cabins, halfway between the Cliff Mine in Keweenaw County and the Quincy Mine in Hancock, until a man named Hulbert discovered the Calumet Conglomerate Lode. He shipped a barrel of the rock with chunks of copper in it to Boston. Thus began the great Calumet and Hecla Mining Company. Houghton County's population, with the villages of Red Jacket, Blue Jacket, Yellow Jacket, numerous other mine locations, and Laurium, grew from 35,389 in the 1890 census to 88,098 in 1910. The town of Red Jacket was later renamed "Calumet" but at the time of the story, it was still "Red Jacket."

The managers of C&H, as well as the other companies, wanted good workers, religious and law-abiding men with families. Mining was hard and dangerous. Many workers would quit as soon as they could find other jobs or buy farmland. The mining companies needed more people willing to work for low wages. From the workers' pay, the company subtracted the cost of their headlamps and other supplies.

Immigrants arrived by the thousands from Finland, Norway, Sweden, Poland, Italy, Germany, and many other countries. Each group had its own church and social agency. These groups helped newly arriving immigrants and kept cultural traditions. People from each nation clung to their own, distrusting the other groups.

As the mines went deeper, companies needed bigger steam engines. These could be built in the rock houses and smelters, but it was much harder to bring machines to the bottom of the mines. Drilling improved from hand drills pounded with sledge hammers to drills using compressed air. These were operated by two men, and "drill boys," who carried water to the drill steels (the moving parts of the drill that grew hot with friction). The drill boys were not actually boys but younger men who were paid less than experienced miners. The worst job was loading the rock into tram cars, and pushing those cars down the stopes, or side tunnels at each level connecting to the shaft. Pushing a tram car required only a strong back, not an understanding of English. So this work was usually done by the newest immigrants. Sometimes they felt like human mules.

Many men died when dynamite exploded at the wrong time or when rock fell from the ceiling which was called a "hanging wall." Sometimes the timbers caught on fire. The cost of copper was estimated at one man dead and two or more hurt or disabled each week.

C&H tried to keep their workers happy. The men and their families could go to a company doctor whenever they needed to for $1.00 a month deducted from their pay. The company built hundreds of small houses and rented them for about $6.00 a month. They gave land for churches, built a library, schools, a hospital, and a public bathhouse with an indoor swimming pool. However, some historians say that building the bath house and pool were cheaper for the company than putting indoor plumbing in hundreds of company houses. Evening classes were available for people to learn English, study to be American citizens, or complete grades seven and eight.

Red Jacket was a "company town." C&H owned almost all the land and houses. Mining was the main industry, so all people depended on it. They either worked for the company or sold goods and services to those who did. Company management often told local government officials, business owners, and newspapers what to do. C&H was like a good parent, but the time comes when children want to stand up on their own.

The nation was changing. A new century brought modern thought, which people began to call the Progressive Movement. The Wright Brothers flew at Kitty Hawk. Socialism, the idea that government should give more services to all people and own major industries, began to grow in Europe. Labor unions began to try to protect the rights of workers. People across the country began to see the need for better public health.

New copper regions opened in Montana and Arizona. These mines produced copper more cheaply. C&H, Quincy and other Michigan companies had to compete. Many different problems caused the 1913 Copper Strike. When the long and violent strike finally ended, community leaders said people should put the strike behind them and look to a better future. It was not easy for people on either side to erase the bitter feelings. Some observers noted that Finns seemed to be the most punished. Although most of them only wanted better working conditions and were not socialists, ill feelings continued. The Finnish Anti-Socialist League formed and grew rapidly to try to get rid of the idea that all Finnish people were socialists. The social and economic costs of the strike were huge.

As Europe entered World War I, the price of copper declined for a time. A few of the mines closed. By 1915, the price of copper rose again, and the area enjoyed a short return to the "boom days." The goal of union representation was not achieved until thirty years later, when C&H recognized the International Union of Mine, Mill and Smelter Workers of the Congress of Industrial Organizations as the bargaining unit for its workers.

Copper mining slowed gradually over the 1920s and 30s. C&H finally stopped all operations as the result of a strike in 1968. Although the population of the area is much lower nearly a century later, *"living on sisu"* is still a good way to describe the people of the entire copper range. Through all its ups and downs, the area remains proud of its special role in the history of the United States. The Keweenaw National Historical Park was established in 1992. Its headquarters are in the former C&H Pay Office on Red Jacket Road across the street from the library. Many historical societies have formed and work to preserve the churches, homes and buildings of the "boom days." Huge flats of stamp sand, which filled in over twenty percent of Torch Lake near the village of Lake Linden, are now covered with native grasses, wild flowers and trees, thanks to being named a Super Fund Clean Up site. The C&H mill office building in Lake Linden is now the home of the Houghton County Historical Museum.

The Italian Hall had to be demolished in 1984 for safety reasons. Now a memorial park stands on the site. On January 26, 1993, *The Daily Mining Gazette* ran an article about an interview with a man identifying himself only as "Bill." He claimed to have witnessed the deathbed confession in the early 1930's from the man who cried "Fire." He told the *Gazette* that two county sheriffs, two judges, an attorney, a priest and an undertaker were present. All swore never to reveal the man's name to protect his family. The witnesses agreed to keep the secret and that only the last of them alive would speak out. "Bill" was the last of the group living in 1993.

According to Bill, the guilty man was about eighteen years old at the time. He had been drinking in the first floor bar. He went up into the hall and yelled, "Fire!" as a joke. He did not run away afterwards, but stayed to help with rescue efforts. He even helped to dig the graves. He feared being lynched if he revealed himself. He later moved, (probably to Baraga) worked in the logging camps, married and raised a family. Bill had known him for about twenty years at the time of his confession. Bill reported that the man was hysterical and crying when he confessed. He had difficulty relating his story and died two days later. He was known in the community for always helping people and volunteering. No one knew his secret and his name remains a mystery.

Many researchers say this and other similar confession stories are false, but a copy of the article remains on file in the Michigan Technological University Archives. Rumors about the cause of the panic were so common some became accepted as fact. Many believed that the doors at the bottom of the steps opened inward. Others argued about the number of people killed. One rumor put the number of dead as high as eighty. More recent research also points to differences between the testimony given at the coroner's inquest and later accounts at the congressional hearings. The most recent, and probably best, conclusion by Steve Letho in his book *Death's Door*, states that it probably was a member of the Citizen's Alliance who entered the hall and shouted **fire**. The purpose would have been to disrupt the party, but not with the direct intention of causing so many deaths in a panic.

Historical People
some of whom interact with, or are mentioned by,
fictional characters in the story

<hr>

Peraley Abbey, Michigan National Guard Commander

Alexander Agassiz, President of Calumet and Hecla
Mining in Boston, MA, from 1871-1910

Rodolphe Agassiz, Vice President of C&H, Boston

Ana Clemenc, "Big Annie," organizer of the Western
Federation of Miners Women's Auxiliary, sometimes called the Copper Country's "Joan of Arc"
in the newspapers

James A. Cruse, Houghton County Sheriff

Clarence Darrow, Western Federation of Miners lawyer

Woodbridge N. Ferris, Governor of Michigan

Charles E. Hietala, secretary/treasurer of the district
WFM

James MacNaughton, General Manager of Calumet and
Helca Mining Company

Charles E. Mahoney, Western Federation of Miners
Vice President

Guy Miller, Western Federation of Miners Executive
Board, editor of *Miner's Bulletin*

John A. Moffitt, United States Bureau of Immigration, assigned by Wilson to work on the Michigan conflict

Moyer, Charles H., WFM President

Patrick H. O'Brien, Circuit Court Judge, known as the "workingman's advocate"

Walter P. Palmer, sent by Moffit as a special investigator

A.E. Petermann, C&H lawyer

Allen Rees, C&H lawyer

Quincy Adams Shaw, Jr., President of C&H during the strike

Roy C. Vanderhook, Major in the Michigan National Guard

James A. Waddell, men of his company were hired by Sheriff Cruse as extra deputies assigned to guard mine property during the strike. These deputies were known as "Waddies" and were considered hired thugs and hated by the strikers.

Research Sources — Photographic Credits

1. Photos labeled: "KNHP-F" are included courtesy of the National Park Service, Keweenaw National Historical Park, Jack Foster Collection
2. Photos labeled: "MTU" are included courtesy of the Michigan Technological University Archives, Houghton, MI
3. Photos labeled: "FAHA" are used courtesy of the Finnish-American Historical Archives, Finlandia University, Hancock, MI.
4. Photo labeled: SV is included courtesy of Superior View, Marquette, MI. www.viewsofthepast.com
5. Photos labeled: "RR" are used courtesy of Ralph Raffaelli's collection.

Special photo note: the initial "N" following any photo used indicates that J. W. Nara, grandfather of Dr. Robert Nara, was the photographer. According to Dr. Nara, it is highly likely that J.W. Nara took the other photos as well. J.W. Nara imprinted many of his photos with his mark, but not all of the thousands of photos he took were marked in this way. Of the unmarked photos which have become part of several collections and archives, the chances are perhaps ninety percent that they are Nara photos, especially those taken of the Calumet area.

To see more Nara photos depicting life in the Copper Country during the early 1900's, consider purchasing Deborah K. Frontiera's book, *Copper Country Chronicler: The Best of J.W. Nara.*

Books

Virginia Law Burns, *Tall Annie: A Biography*, ISBN 0-9604726-3-0, Enterprise Press, 8600 S. Fenner Rd., Lansing, MI. 1987

Joseph Damrell, Ed., *Isaac Polvi: The Autobiography of a Finnish Immigrant*, ISBN 0-87839-066-9, North Star Press, P.O. Box 451, St. Cloud, MN. 1991

Dave Engel and Gerry Mantel, *Calumet: Copper Country Metropolis*, ISBN 0-9722292-0-5, River City Memoirs, 5597 Third Av., Rudolph, WI. 55475. 2002

Armask E. Homio, *History of Finns in Michigan*, Wayne State University Press, Detroit, MI. Finlandia University, Hancock, MI. 2001

Larry Lankton, *Cradle to Grave: Life, Work and Death at the Lake Superior Copper Mines*, ISBN0-19-508357-1, Oxford University Press, 198 Madison Ave., New York, NY. 10016. 1991

Amanda Wiljanen Larson, *Finnish Heritage in America*, a Bicentennial Publication of Delta Chapter. The Delta Kappa Gamma Society, Marquette, MI. 1976

Steve Letho, *Death's Door*, Momentum Books, L.L. C., 2145 Crooks Rd., Suite 208, Troy, MI. 48084. 2006.

James Medved, *Swedetown: The History of the Location Just South of Calumet, Michigan*, James Medved, Milwaukee and Swedetown, with Regin Heliste, Swedetown, 1983

Molloy, Larry, *Italian Hall: The Witnesses Speak*, An analysis of the Houghton County Corner's Inquest into the tragedy at the Italian Hall, Calumet, MI, December 24, 1913. Great Lakes GeoScience, Hubbell, MI. 2004

Jerry Stanley, *Big Annie of Calumet: A True Story of the Industrial Revolution*, ISBN 0-517-70098-0, Crown Publishers Inc., a Random House Company, 201 E. 50th St., New York, NY. 10022. 1996

Arthur W. Thurner: *Calumet, Copper and People, History of a Michigan Mining Community, 1864-1970,* privately published. 1974. Available in most regional bookstores and libraries.

Rebels on the Range, The Michigan Copper Miners' Strike of 1913-1914, John H. Forster Press, a Division of the Houghton County Historical Society, Lake Linden, MI. 1984, 1998, 1999

Strangers and Sojourners, A History of Michigan's Keweenaw Peninsula, ISBN 0-8143-2396-0 Wayne State University Press, Detroit, MI 1994

Agencies

Keweenaw National Historical Park, 25947 Red Jacket Rd.,
Calumet, MI 49913; 906-337-1104

Michigan Technological University Archives, J. Robert VanPelt
Library, 1400 Townsend Dr., Houghton, MI 49931, 906-
487-2505

The Finnish American National Historic Archive and Museum,
Finlandia University, Hancock, MI 49930; 906-487-7301

The South Range Historical Museum, South Range, Michigan

Index for Living on Sisu

union 5, 16, 21, 23, 25, 28, 43,
   47-8, 51, 55-6, 59, 61-2, 68-9,
   73, 77-8, 80, 85-6, 90, 92, 106,
   121, 127-8, 130, 135, 139, 141,
   144, 146-8, 153, 156-7, 164,
   173, 177, 182, 213
vanhapojan kääntiä 38-9
vihta 46, 118, 176
viiliä 8
voi tuhanen 121
Waddell, James A., Waddies 80, 90,
   102, 130, 156, 199
Western Federation of Miners,
   WFM 5, 16, 21, 26, 44, 47, 55,
   58, 62, 68, 70, 73, 78, 86, 88,
   92-4, 97, 100, 102, 106, 109,
   119-20, 124, 137, 141, 144,
   146, 148, 153, 156, 158, 185,
   199, 201, 207, 209
widow-maker 25

Made in the USA
Charleston, SC
09 November 2014